C

EVERY STEP
YOU TAKE

PAN ORIGINAL

First published 1993 by Pan Macmillan Children's Books

a division of Pan Macmillan Publishers Limited
Cavaye Place London SW10 9PG
and Basingstoke

Associated companies throughout the world

ISBN 0-330-32844-1

1 3 5 7 9 8 6 4 2

A CIP catalogue record for this book is available from
the British Library

Typeset by Cambridge Composing (UK) Limited, Cambridge
Printed by Cox & Wyman Ltd, Reading

For Terry and Catrin who made it possible,
and Rachel for the trouble she took

Chapter 1

It was still as cold as night in the tall room; but grey light was coming in through dusty diamond-paned windows, set high in the stone walls. The room contained the quiet emptiness of a place where no one lives. A place that people visit hurriedly for some purpose but do not stay. There was dust on everything, on the narrow table and benches which skirted the walls, on the bookshelves and books toppled in piles. Black cloaks and vestments hung like folded stone, flowing down in frozen layers into shapeless solidity.

A small sound came from somewhere in the church beyond the room. The hairs crept on the back of his head, his ears turned towards the sound, his hand flicked. Still he stared down. Toes showed like a row of marbles protruding from the black mass in the corner. Some had red streaks on them, like his favourite marble from when he was a kid. He never swapped that one, never even used it to play with, it had been his best one. He bent down. The toes were as cold and smooth as the marbles of his childhood. Some of the red came away on his hand.

He sighed and pulled the pile of cassocks down to hide the foot. When all was tidy again he let himself out of the vestry door and into the graveyard. It was misty now, the grass grey with dew, but it would be a nice day later.

He looked around. It was a pity, he thought, he would have liked to have done things properly. He knew where there were a couple of soft spots that could have been

1

easily dug. He'd seen them working there last week. Still, it was too late now. He'd stayed with her too long. The sun would be up soon and people would be about. He had to go.

An hour later he was on the road, in the open country-side. He had left the small town behind. He stuck out his thumb as cars whined up and passed. He never turned to look at them or showed surprise when they did not stop. No one seemed to want to offer him a lift, but it did not matter. He headed purposefully along. He knew where he was going. It was the only place left for him to go.

The Verger sat down heavily. He nearly slipped off the narrow pew and, in pushing himself back up, he jarred his knee and bruised his hip. He didn't even notice. His heart was beating very fast and he held his hand over his mouth to seal in the vomit.

As soon as he came in, he'd seen that some idiot had left all the cassocks piled up anyhow, left the place in a real mess. He had hurried over to sort it out, as if he hadn't got enough to do. First Saturday in May, one of their busiest times. And it was going to be a lovely day. The first ceremony was at nine-thirty. And he had found . . .

He'd never seen anything like it, not in real life. In films – but then you knew it wasn't real. On the News sometimes, when they didn't move the camera away quickly enough, and you saw something you weren't supposed to see in what was left of a house or lying in the streets. Something that was still wearing torn denim or bits of shirt but looked like a ragged lump of meat.

He forced himself to look again at what he had uncovered. The girl lay on a bed of black robes. Arms and legs grew out like grotesque stamens, crooked and bent away from the centre. Her body opened out like a huge peony, blossoming red.

His mind jumped to the cars arriving, the brides getting out, the photographers, the families and guests. He could see all the waiting buffets and cakes and champagne in hotels and halls and marquees all over the town. He imagined the reverberations pulsing through so many people's lives. Their most important day, ruined by this.

He covered it over. No one had to go in there. No one. He quickly gathered what was needed for the morning's services and then he hurried out, locking the door behind him.

The Verger need not have worried. It all went perfectly well. Bells pealed the news of wedding after wedding across the town. Confetti was thrown, and faces were frozen for ever, grouped and smiling, in the bright May sunshine. The choir sang and the organ played a requiem for the girl whose life had flowed out of her that morning and soaked into the cold stone floor. She would never marry. She was part of the fabric of the church now, cold and carved as marble.

Chapter 2

Chris O'Neill woke suddenly and wondered where they were. She was fed up with this trip already and it hadn't even got started. What was she doing, sitting here heading for the middle of Wales, the middle of nowhere? The bus ride was interminable. The noise and the people were closing in on her, getting on her nerves. Big mistake. She didn't know a crampon from a tampon and was terrified of heights. What she knew about Outdoor Pursuits could be written on the stamp of the postcard home. She was here because of Anna, because Anna had asked her to come.

Anna sprawled next to her, mouth slightly open, her body loose with sleep. Her Walkman dinned away to itself. Chris reached over and turned it off.

'Hey – I was listening to that!'

'Sorry,' Chris said. 'I thought you were asleep.'

Anna turned her head away into the bus window.

'. . . wondered if you would like a drink?'

Chris stared up at tiny images of herself, twinned in mirror glasses.

'Sorry. Who? Who wondered?'

'Andy – Andy wondered if you girls would like a drink.'

'No. Thank you, Mark. You can tell Andrew that we are not thirsty.'

Mark ambled back to his place at the back with the lads. Andrew Henderson received the news impassively. He secured the Coca-Cola bottle between his interlocked ankles and stared straight ahead, sipping a can of Carlsberg.

In the bus's large rear-view mirror, Chris watched him watching her. That was another thing. Chris's mind travelled back to the last service station.

'It's all right, love.' The girl on the checkout till had sounded different, they were moving to another part of the country. 'That lad's just paid for yours.'

Andy and Mark had been in front of them in the queue. Anna had grinned at her. Andy hadn't even looked back. What was that all about?

Chris yawned at the anonymous countryside slipping past. Could be anywhere. How much longer was it going to take?

Andy was OK but she didn't think she really fancied him. Plenty did. He had American good looks: chiselled features, wheat-blond hair, but he used too much gel on it and she didn't like his haircut. She checked out his muscular, compact body, that was nice enough. Legs were a bit on the short side, though. He was captain of practically every school team going, another reason not to fancy him. Anyway, he had a girlfriend – Elaine Something in the Sixth Form. Diane fancied him like mad. His eyes met Chris's in the mirror and she looked quickly away.

Diane was sitting on her own now. Michaela, her best friend, had been moved to the front of the bus. Ms Steadman had refused to stop again for her to wander around on the verge searching like a cat for somewhere to vomit. Michaela was sitting next to the driver, her head buried in a plastic bag. Diane was peering into a small hand mirror, retouching her make-up, the contents of her make-up bag strewn across the vacant seat. Chris could not see the pack of multi-coloured condoms that she knew

5

the bag contained. Diane braced herself against the jolting and swaying of the bus to apply a second layer of mascara. She liked to make the most of herself.

Chris considered going along and talking to her, Di could be a good laugh, but she couldn't be bothered to move. Anna was still asleep and the only people within easy range were Natalie Turner and Colin Grogan. Natalie sat alone, picking at the thick pads of scar tissue around her non-existent fingernails, sometimes she gnawed at them a bit. She was muttering to herself, but Chris could not hear what she was saying.

Colin half-heartedly waved a packet of crisps in Chris's direction. He looked relieved when she shook her head, she didn't like salt and vinegar. Half a hand of bananas stuck out of his bag like a baseball mitt and the wrappers of all he had consumed so far rustled around his feet. He had started unwrapping his sandwiches before they were out of the school gates. He stared out of the window now, consuming crisps at a steady pace, pushing them into his face. He was sitting as far away from Andy and the lads as he could possibly get. He could not be looking forward to this weekend much. Chris wondered what he was doing here. She wondered again what *she* was doing here. You didn't have to be interested in Outdoor Pursuits to come on this trip, but she imagined it probably helped. Anna had wanted her to come, and it was a chance to get away for a couple of days. These had seemed good enough reasons.

An empty lager can rattled past from the back and joined Colin's crisp bags. The radio screamed out from the front of the bus: 'Newsbeat Newsbeat'. They had all clamoured for Radio One but no one was listening now. Chris put her Walkman on and searched backwards and

6

forwards for someone to tell her what it was like to be in love. She closed her eyes.

Andrew Henderson watched the thick fair wavy hair push back from her face and when her head disappeared from his view, he was happy just to stare at her long legs stretching out into the aisle of the minibus.

The lorry driver glanced over to his companion and then back at the road. Although it was against company rules, he often picked up hitchhikers. It could get lonely on a long run, but so far this guy had said nothing. He reached out and turned on the radio. The silence was getting on his nerves.

'This is *The World at One* with Charles Hutchins. Now the news headlines . . .'

'Don't mind, do you?' the driver said. 'It's just I like to listen to the radio on a long trip – for company, like. I don't listen to music – like to hear people talking.'

'. . . Police searching for sixteen-year-old Angela Bingham have indicated that they are becoming increasingly fearful for her safety . . .'

'No, go ahead,' his passenger said. 'I don't mind at all.'

'. . . alerted after Angela failed to return from . . .'

'Smoke?' The driver lit a cigarette and waved the packet in his direction.

'No – no thanks.'

'The teenager, described as pretty with long dark hair and brown eyes, was last seen . . .'

'Like to listen to the news – keep up with things, know what I mean?'

'Despite intense police activity, there are still no clues as yet to . . .'

7

The driver checked his side mirror and edged out around an old van, the big steering-wheel sliding round and back again under his hands. Tattoos snaked up his arms and disappeared under the sleeves of his shirt.

'Terrible, isn't it? Young girls and women – not safe for them to go out alone.'

'Yeah – terrible.' His passenger agreed and then stared out of the cab window at the high hedges sliding past.

'Got a girl of my own. That's her up there, with the wife.' The driver glanced up at a fading Polaroid wedged above the mirror with the penants and rosary beads. 'With me away a lot, nights too, I drive nights sometimes, I worry.' He looked over for some response. He strained to listen but his passenger stared straight ahead. 'I worry a lot.'

'Police are now widening their search to . . .'

The driver slammed his rig into another gear as they started climbing up into the hills.

They hadn't found her then. He hoped she'd be safe where he'd put her – for a while at least. It was a shame that he hadn't been able to do a proper job – lay her to rest properly. He'd picked out a lovely spot, she'd have had flowers and everything. It made him angry when things did not turn out right. This guy going on about his wife and kid. He looked up at the curling Polaroid. Fat cow. And the kid, she was quite pretty now but she'd turn into a fat cow like her mother in a few years' time – you could see it in her face. Not a patch on his Angie (he called her 'Angie', no one else did, it was special to him), not in her class. Angie was really beautiful. He watched her. In his mind he watched her. She was walking away from him, legs long and tanned in rolled-up shorts. She was wearing a T-shirt. She turned, flicking back her long black hair, waved and smiled right at him.

When he first came back, he couldn't believe how much she'd changed. Even as a little kid playing in the neighbourhood, she had been something special, but in the time he'd been away, she had turned into a beautiful woman. He had worried he wouldn't be able to stay there, near her – but getting a job had not been as difficult as he'd thought. There was still development going on in the growing town and you could keep yourself to yourself. They didn't ask questions on the sites, not if you could do the job. And he was a good worker, he could turn his hand to anything. Strong too. Worked out every day. He'd found a good place to live, not big, but big enough for him. And private, the old bag downstairs just let him alone.

Pretty soon he was seeing her every single day and really getting to know her like never before: what she did, where she went, who her friends were. He felt really close to her, knowing if she was happy or sad at a glance. He got to know and love every changing expression, every mood on her face. He knew every move she made. She had been unfaithful and that had upset him for a while, but he made himself see that he had been away and it was understandable so he had forgiven her. It would change now he was back for good and could be there for her and see her all the time. He mustn't let jealousy spoil it, he had told himself.

'This money business in football – ruining the game. Making it so the ordinary fan going to a game on a Sat'dy don't matter any more. Spurs is my team.' The driver looked over. 'You got a team at all?'

But his passenger seemed to have gone to sleep. His body was twisted away into the window, his hands tightly clasped between his thighs. His eyes were screwed shut and his face, set in rigid lines, was wet. He was scratched up bad on that side, looked like a cat or something had been at him, or maybe he'd been in an accident.

'That's right – you have a kip.' The driver lit another cigarette. 'We all need a good kip, sometimes.'

He wound down the window to let some fresh air in. Funny smell in the cab, like when he drove for G. & B. Purveyors to the Trade – Quality Meat.

'I'll have to be dropping you off soon, mate,' the driver said to himself.

Chapter 3

'See you then,' Chris said, but Anna had already left the room.

Chris stretched out on the bed and stared up at the ceiling, tracing pictures in the web of cracks that led from the window to the damp patch in the opposite corner. She used to pretend she could fly to the ceiling when she was a kid, and look down on herself on the bed.

She did not like this miles-from-anywhere place. The grey house squatted at the bottom of a valley, the windows opened out on to hills stacked away in ranks. It was oppressive, claustrophobic. The hills cut the day short, even now the house was in shadow. A choked and neglected garden crept up to two sides of the house and a stand of dark firs hung over the end gable and outhouses. Chris was glad they had not been put in there. Their room was at the front of the house overlooking a steep, eroded driveway of splintered slate.

Inside the house was scuffed and battered. It was pretty basic, but that didn't bother her. There was something sad about this place. It seemed exhausted, worn out by the number of people who used it. It had once been a home and now it was a hostel. People came and went and didn't care. High up on the walls of the hall and staircase you could see pretty, faded flower-pattern wallpaper, lower down it had been worn away and replaced by an uneven band of greasy dirt. Here and there were remnants of the house's former life, but for the most part the furnishings were bland and institutional, in every room the same.

Chris was glad when Anna had gone. She liked to have time to get used to new places and she wanted time to think. Anna had been restless to check the place out, see what was going on. Chris had just lain on her bed, wrapped in a towel after her shower, watching Anna unpack and put all her things away. Anna was very neat and tidy, something that surprised people who didn't know her very well. While she opened drawers and put things on hangers she kept up a constant barrage of nagging about Chris wasting time, not caring about things, being untidy and messy. She'd even wanted her towel back. Finally she had given up and gone out.

Chris sighed, time to get up and get dressed properly. Cold was seeping into the room from the thick stone walls. She thought about Anna as she sorted through her clothes. They were so different, in looks, interests, temperament, everything.

Anna was as dark as Chris was fair. She wore her hair long, thick black waves curled and snaked down to her shoulders, framing her oval face. Her eyes were almost black and always seemed to be assessing, taking in impressions but giving nothing back. Her thick brows were often drawn together into a single bar which made her look hostile, almost forbidding, and her full, finely shaped mouth seemed less at home with a smile than a sneer. People didn't mess with her, that was for sure. Most of them regarded her with an uneasy combination of envy and fear. Even the sports she excelled at tended to be solitary. She was naturally athletic and liked to compete and win, but she was as happy competing against herself as against other people. Climbing was her current favourite thing. That's why they were here.

Chris would not have described herself as athletic. She regarded physical activity with a mixture of guilt and indifference, and as for climbing, heights made her seriously scared. So what *was* she doing here? There were so many contrasts between them that people found it difficult to understand why they were friends. Sometimes, like now, Chris found it difficult herself. She didn't usually like to think too much about it, in case she picked it apart and found there was nothing there. They had been friends since the first day of the first year at secondary school, thrown together by one of those accidents. Chris was sitting next to a space – someone had to fill the seat. As Michaela was on holiday the someone was Anna. They had been sitting next to each other ever since. Chris could not explain why she had worked so hard to win over the grave little girl who seldom smiled and rarely said anything, why she had wanted so much to break down her reserve. Chris was different. She made friends easily; open-faced with a ready smile, wanting to be liked, eager to please. She had sensed that Anna's reticence was not shyness. It was more an indifference to other people. She genuinely didn't care. This had intrigued Chris and filled her with a feeling that was uncomfortably close to envy, made her want to get near and make her care.

And it had worked. Gradually the reserve had broken down and Chris had been allowed in. Chris smiled to herself, it had not been a wasted effort. Chris still felt honoured; that this friendship, so hard won, so exclusive, was a privilege. It set Anna apart from everybody else.

When Chris had finished dressing she still didn't want to join other people, so she rummaged in her backpack and brought out her diary, thinking of things to say for today, things to put down. The diary opened at the beginning of March, at the page where she had written down what she felt, or was beginning to feel, for Nick. She hadn't even told Anna. She did not want Anna's penetrating common sense and ferocious realism corroding it, although she thought that she had probably guessed. She would have to be pretty stupid not to, and Anna was very far from that. The ordinary world had faded to monochrome as thoughts and fantasies about Nick Stephens filled her head and the pages of her diary. She put down her pen and began to read. She had not known what he felt, but that didn't seem to matter. She wanted him and she was going to get him. It was all a matter of timing and she had her plans.

Everything in the last entries centred on turning this fantasy into reality. An intense and exultant excitement grabbed her throat as she flipped through to the last written pages and started to read:

Thursday 29th April

School Disco – a dismal non-event: *not this time*!

I hear Anna in the hall, jingling keys and change in her pocket, impatient – she hates to be kept waiting. She looks up as I come down. Looks away and back and clears her throat and says, quiet and serious, 'You look fantastic.' I grin. I know.

We make it out before my dad sees me and on the way we stop at the Off Licence to buy some vodka. Anna sends me in to buy it, says I look the oldest, that's when I know it is going to work. At the bottom of the school drive she hands me the bottle. 'Here,' she says, 'take a drink. Take two. You'll need it.' I don't think so but I swig it down anyway.

We have our hands stamped and struggle in through the mob of younger kids who always seem

14

to hang round the door. We ignore all the turning heads, or pretend we do. Someone's draped crêpe paper over the scabby white dinner tables stacked with cans and crisps, and coloured lights flash on and off to let you know it's a disco.

Anna says, 'There's Nick,' and grins, as if I hadn't seen him as soon as we got in there! 'He's seen you,' she says – couldn't really miss me. The music is pounding but there aren't many people out on the floor. I dance over towards Nick. His eyebrows creep up, but he doesn't say a thing. Di, Michaela, Anna and me moved into the middle – we're going to put on a real show. Mark comes over to join us. None of the other boys are dancing yet. I try not to look, but every time I turn, I see Nick standing there, drinking a Coke, watching over the rim.

He shakes his head and smiles to himself. He pushes his glasses up his nose, puts down the can and boosts himself off the pillar and heads towards the dance floor.

I feel the touch on my shoulder, like a burn. Lights slide across his Buddy Holly glasses. I can't see his eyes. He shouts something, but I can't hear, he shrugs and dances away and back again, ultra-violet light picking up the white of his shirt. He's tall, thin and gangly, but he dances well. He doesn't fold up into his body and just jerk around like most boys, and he's not showy and macho like Mark. He moves with the music.

Even when we aren't dancing, we don't talk much. He buys me a Coke and we stand so close I can feel the heat of his body on my bare arm. I can hardly breathe. It's getting crowded now, sweaty and hot. He goes to get more Cokes and I go and check out the toilets, choking on cigarette smoke and hairspray, mirror to mirror make-up, every wash-basin taken, someone throwing up – business as usual in there. I pray he'll be waiting for me.

When I get back the DJ is saying it's the last dance, the slow one. I look around but can't see Nick. I'm just starting to panic when his hand takes mine and his arms go around me. He fits me to him as we move to the music. His shirt is sticking to his back, I feel the muscles move under the material, under the skin. He whispers something, I can't quite catch what he's saying. His breath is warm on my neck, I breathe in sweet sweat and after-shave. Other couples drift past draped in streamers and party poppers and silly string. Coloured lights wander in sequence over everything. He kisses me for a long time. I want it to last for ever. I want the record never to stop.

The song ends and the DJ signs off. The lights go up and we eventually break apart. Ms Steadman grins at us as she goes past toting a bin-bag. It's back to being the school hall – stacks of chairs and exam desks, bits of Open Evening display work falling down with the temporary disco decorations. The same as usual. Back to reality. But it's not. He doesn't let go of my hand as we find our coats and he puts his arm round me as we make our way out. We go past Anna, leaning against a pillar, talking to Mark. She raises her eyebrows and smiles – giving me her don't do anything I wouldn't do look.

We walk home with our arms round each other, kicking through cherry blossom, past TV lights flickering from uncurtained windows. When we get to our house we skirt round dad's car and he leads

16

me to the dark space between the porch and the garage. He takes off his glasses, clicks them shut and puts them in his top pocket. He smiles, not saying anything, and tucks some hair behind my ear. He kisses me again, not harder but different than before, my mouth opens to his. He holds my head, fingers barely touching the skin, feathering back through my hair. My own breathing and my heart beating seem to fill the space between us. I have never been kissed like this.

A door slams and next door's dog starts barking. We move apart. He looks down at me but it's too dark to read his smile. I feel slightly stupid with the kiss, with showing too much. Neither of us says anything. We do not know each other like this. He puts his glasses back on and goes to the porch light to check his watch. He asks me what I'm doing at the weekend. I stare at the coconut matting and tell him I'll be away on the trip to Plas Y Defaid. His lips brush mine, and he says, 'See you, then.'

I watch him go. He waves once before he disappears behind next door's hedge. Their dog starts up again, our curtains twitch. I turn to fumble my key into the lock. The last kiss was the merest touch but it burns on my mouth.

I want to (This part is heavily deleted)
I am shocked at myself

Friday 30th April

Nothing!
Too tired.
Too depressed.
Too busy packing.
To write anything.

Chris turned to the next page and picked up her pen.

Saturday 1st May

Just read through Thursday. Feel the same – but
+ + + + + + + + more. He asked me out!
Actually came right out and asked me! And I'm
here! Nick Stephens asks me out the only weekend I
go away. Now *that* is just my luck.
So far today . . .

Chris looked at the rest of the page and chewed her pen.
The long journey here had been so boring that she didn't
want to write about it. Except for one thing. She wiped
the end of the pen on her shirt and began to write.

On the way here I had this feeling that someone was
watching me. Nothing spectacular, but enough to
make me aware of him. Andrew Henderson. I don't
really know him, I know who he is – that's about it.
God, I hope he doesn't fancy me because I don't
fancy him at all! I hope this isn't going to be a
complication. Still, it's only a couple of days, there
won't be enough time for anything much to happen.

Chapter 4

'We're at Saunders' place now. It's on the main street – over.'

D.I. Wainwright eased himself up from the floor where he had been squatting, sifting through a pile of magazines, and raked his hair back. His untidy dark hair was streaked with grey and his knees had gone off like gun shots when he stood up – getting too old for Saturday football. It was only an end of season kickabout, but he hadn't been sorry to be called off the field. If that verger had let on earlier he wouldn't even have been out on the park and they might have stood a chance of nailing the bastard.

'No – no – he's not. Over.'

He listened to the words crackling out of the radio and looked round the room. He didn't have much, but what he had was nice stuff. CD stack, TV and video – probably stolen – have to check the numbers – get him for that as well, with any luck. His lip curled. Tapes and CDs skittered across the floor – Heavy Metal, Hi-Energy, Rap and House, some of that whining poof music. Terrible taste in music. He tipped up a cassette shell, Police. He smiled to himself. Now what did you make of that? They had found cameras in the wardrobe, a good one with the lenses for it, and a small compact, plus binoculars. Quite a little cache he'd got here.

He glanced around the rest of the room. Nothing. The room was almost bare except for his expensive collection of electrical equipment. No pictures, no photographs, no ornaments. The guy was real tidy. Even the bed was neatly made.

''Course not. The old dear downstairs let us in. Over. Yes. Over.'

He listened for a moment, pushing a weight backwards and forwards with his foot.

'Well, nothing much. Fancies himself as a bit of an amateur photographer. No. Not yet. No pics either. Over.'

He'd expected magazines at least. *Knave*, *Penthouse*, corner-shop titles, maybe some harder stuff. But all they'd found so far were body building magazines, straight ones, and a copy of this week's *TV Times*.

'Yeah. But it's all films and fitness stuff.' He toed a video cassette box. 'No hard gear.' He paused. The Superintendent's distorted voice crackled around him. 'I still think he's our boy, though. Just feel it. Hang on, Wendy's found something. Get back to you. Over and out.'

He went over to W.D.C. Wendy Townsend, crouched on the floor in the corner where the dirty carpet met ancient cracked lino. There was a definite bulge beneath the surface. She eased up the flooring and revealed a chaos of photographs. Wainwright spread them out with his pen.

'They don't look to be of anything much, do they?' W.D.C. Townsend said finally. 'Just snaps of the church and street scenes. Maybe he was just trying out his new camera.'

Wainwright nodded absently. He had begun to separate a number of photographs from the rest. He studied the photo of Angela Bingham he'd been given at the briefing. The image was blurred by hasty mass duplication but it was the same girl all right. There she was coming out of the church, and there crossing the road by Woolworths, and again waiting for the school bus. In each one she had been singled out of the crowd by the camera so that, although she appeared to be with a whole mass of people, she was really on her own.

'Hang on, Sir. There's something else under here.'

A thin margin of white showed along the edge of the lino. Using her fingernails like tweezers, W.D.C. Townsend carefully extricated another photograph. Wainwright bent forward to examine it. It was different from the others. Small, less than a postcard but bigger than a contact print, and black and white. A photo of a house, big and built of stone by the look of it, standing by itself. The photograph was so faded that the surrounding hills looked like clouds above it. Two figures stood on the drive in front of the door. Maybe a man and a woman, but cracks travelled across and through them, rendering them unrecognizable.

'Well done, Wend,' he said, grinning at her. 'We'll make a detective of you yet.'

He got up slowly and took out his radio.

'Wainwright, here. We've found some stuff that could be interesting. We're bringing it in.'

He flicked the radio off and replaced it in his top pocket. Between them they expertly edged the evidence into plastic wallets, W.D.C. Townsend cracking shut the sealing strips. Then they left, leaving the room as they'd found it.

Wainwright got into the car and struggled into his seat belt, cursing. They could have had Saunders by now. As it was, God knows how long it would take to find him or what he would get up to before they did. It was all down to that stupid old verger.

Saunders was known all right. He'd been in the frame

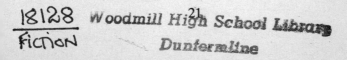

a couple of times, but never for anything as bad as this. They'd never had enough to make anything stick but he didn't like this guy, had a bad feeling about him. Guys like him were a real menace. They should have put him away last time when they had the chance. A muscle jumped in his cheek as the girl's face came back to him and with it other images. She had been such a pretty kid. He pushed his hair out of his eyes and scowled out at the road. It didn't matter how often you were called upon to deal with it, you never got used to it. Not really.

He took out the small black and white photograph and smoothed out its transparent plastic casing. The others were interesting but predictable. They would add to the circumstantial. This was the one that was important. He examined it carefully. Photographs got worn and creased like that from being carried all the time in a pocket or a wallet. This place had to be significant. Then something snagged in his memory. One of the checks they'd run on Saunders had turned something up. Now he remembered. He'd been picked up a couple of times for breaking and entering, but he hadn't been done for it because the house was a derelict property. Now where the hell had it been?

W.D.C. Townsend looked over from the driver's seat. 'Are you going to check on that place or leave it to the local police?'

'Got to find out where it is first,' Wainwright replied, preoccupied.

'It's called Plas Y Defaid,' she said as she started the engine. 'And it looks like it could be north Wales.'

'How do you know that?' Wainwright glanced up in surprise.

'Because that's what it says on the back of the photo-

'graph,' she said, grinning at him as she reversed the car.

Shoppers jumped at the snarl of the siren and motorists made way as the police car pulled out from the pavement and edged into the stream of Saturday traffic.

Chapter 5

Chris quickly put the diary back in her bag when she heard the tentative knock on the door. She didn't know who to expect but it was Natalie Turner standing there, hair soaked and dangling down in straggly ringlets.

'Hi, Nat. What can I do for you?'

She didn't exactly ask her in, but Natalie was under her arm anyway and questing about the room like a terrier.

'Youse got a hair drier? I'd have brought mine but it's broke.'

'Yeah, sure. Anna's travel drier is around here somewhere.'

Chris came back with a bright green light-weight drier. Anna never went anywhere without it, well, not anywhere she was likely to get her hair wet. She handed it to Natalie, expecting her to go away now. Within seconds vicious whirring filled the room.

'No, hang on, Natalie.' Chris went over to her. She had it on the highest setting and unbearably close to her head. 'It'll all frizz up if you do it like that. Here, let me do it.'

'Would you really?' Natalie turned the drier and caught Chris full in the face.

'Sure. Why not?' Chris blinked into the mirror. 'First of all it's too wet. Towel it a bit and we'll put on some mousse.'

Natalie fingered a cold sore at the corner of her mouth. 'This is ever so painful, Chris,' she said. 'You got any stuff?'

'Yeah, but first things first,' Chris said, scrunching

24

mousse into the damp hair and working the drier back and forth. 'Don't finger it. You'll make it worse.'

Chris flicked off the drier and Natalie's plain face peered out from a mass of brown curls. She tentatively pushed at them with a pudgy nail-bitten hand. She looked up at Chris towering over her, brush in one hand, drier in the other, smiling down at her handiwork.

'Thanks, Chris.' She pushed at her hair again. 'It looks great!'

Chris smiled. 'That's OK. No problem.' She turned and walked to the chest of drawers. 'You've got really pretty hair, you know.'

Natalie watched her in the mirror and then looked down at herself. She pulled at her shirt. It was getting too tight for her and gaped a bit. There was no point complaining to Mum, she would just say it was puppy fat, but Natalie was no longer so sure about that.

'Don't look so sad,' Chris said coming back. 'Here, dab some of this on that sore spot – it's really good.'

Natalie daubed at herself with the swab of blue sharp-smelling liquid. 'Oooh, Chris!' she squealed. 'It really stings!'

'And now . . .'

Chris's face was next to hers. Natalie studied what the other girl saw: little curranty eyes, too close together in a fat face, stared back. She took in forehead, cheeks and chin. Even if she gave up chocolate, fatty food, and used special face wash, it never seemed to get rid of all of them. Her gaze slid over to the greeny-blue eyes that were appraising her; to Chris's even features, the wide mouth curling into a slight smile, teeth white and perfect. Chris had a lot of freckles but no spots. Natalie's little parrot mouth pouched even more. It was not fair. Chris was really pretty, even this close up.

'Put some of this stuff on.' Chris handed her concealer. 'Now rub it in.'

'You look so pretty when you smile like that,' Natalie said quietly.

'Don't be daft!' Chris turned away to hide the colour rising in her face. She set out make-up on the top of the cupboard. 'We'll make you look great!'

It took quite a time and was tricky. More than once Chris wished that she hadn't started, but finally she turned Natalie round.

'What do you think?'

Natalie looked at the stranger in the mirror with surprise and delight. She didn't have to say anything. Her face was enough. Chris put her make-up things back in the drawer.

'Hey, Chris, do you know what?' Natalie suddenly said. It was what she had come in for really, before she'd got side-tracked.

'No. What?'

'Do you know why that lot were so late?'

'What lot?'

'Peters and that lot.'

'No.' Chris shrugged. 'Didn't know they were.'

'Oooh, yes. Ever so.' Natalie's eyes gleamed. She loved telling people things. Usually they'd heard it before and told her to shut up, or they told her to shut up anyway, but Chris wouldn't do that. She had something really good to tell and she knew from her face that Chris didn't know a thing about it. 'They were stopped by the police!'

'So?'

'So?' Natalie repeated the word, puzzled, and then settled to tell her, lowering her voice and whispering to be part of the drama. 'The police stopped them because they're looking for a murderer!'

She delivered the last word with a flourish and a little thrill in her voice. Her curls bobbed as she sat back, ready for further interrogation.

'Where? On the bus?'

Chris imagined him, crouched and desperate, under the seats with the empty cans and crisp packets while everyone above laughed and shouted and carried on, unaware of the danger lurking in their midst. Or horizontal and rigid, hiding in one of the canoes on the trailer behind.

'No!' Natalie looked at Chris carefully, not sure if she was taking the mickey. 'Don't be silly! They didn't think he was on the bus or anything.' She let out a pekinese sneeze of a laugh. 'They stopped Mr Peters to warn him!' She was suddenly wide-eyed and serious. 'There's been a murder – and the murderer is heading this way!'

'What do you mean?' Chris seemed to wake up to what she was being told. 'How do you know this, anyway?'

'Heard Peters telling Steadman.' Natalie grinned and hugged her knees, happy that her words had finally struck home. 'Scary – isn't it?'

When Chris decided it was time to be sociable, it wasn't hard to find where her friends were. The music drew her to them like a directional beacon. Dave made room for her on the floor by the window, and started to tell her the news.

'Yeah, I heard,' she said. 'Natalie told me.'

'Christ, how did she know?' Dave said, angrily. 'That was our story!'

Chris shrugged. 'She knows everything. Heard Peters telling Steadman about it.'

'Yeah? Well,' Dave countered, 'Gary and me were on the bus.'

27

'Is it true, then? This murderer stuff?' Anna leant forward trying to hear them through the tape.

'We heard it. Didn't we, Gaz?'

Gary was stretched out on the floor next to Andrew. He looked even taller lying down. His trainers, trailing luminous laces, dwarfed the waste-paper basket and his track suit seemed to contain a lot of empty space.

'Did you see Natalie earlier?' He propped himself up and sniggered. 'All that clowny make-up? What a dog!'

'So? What happened?' Anna directed her questioning at Dave.

'Well, we were hammering along and I was sort of dozing, right? And we started to slow down. I say to Gaz: What's happening? he goes: Filth have stopped Peters for speeding. I go: Don't be daft he can't have been doing more than fifty. It won't do more than fifty! He says: Different limits here. So I say: There aren't any limits here – it's nowhere, man!' Dave stopped to laugh a little at his own joke. 'Anyway, by then this guy's tapping Peters' window and he's winding it down. Gaz says: So? Filth got him anyway. And he heard that!' Dave laughed again. 'You were bricking it! He gave you a real hard look.'

'So?' Gary's eyes filmed with sulky aggression. 'What do I care? Bet he wasn't even a cop!'

'Don't be so stupid. 'Course he bleeding was! If he wasn't a copper what was he then? I saw him downstairs with Peters, just now, so he's got to be!'

'Well? What happened? What did he say?' Anna was impatient to get the rest of the story before these two lost it in one of their squabbles.

'Well, this guy says his name is Wainwright and he flashes some sort of ID . . .'

'Could have been anything,' Gary interrupted. 'Could have been his credit card. Peters is such a sap.'

'Oh, shut up Gary! Go on, Dave.'

'I couldn't hear everything but it seemed to come down to this. Some guy topped this bird and he's heading this way.'

'You mean,' Anna was still seeking more clarification than she knew she was likely to get, 'to this area?'

'No, he doesn't.' Gary lolled over, grinning. 'He means to here. To this house.'

Chapter 6

'Here, Anna.' Chris knew she wasn't asleep. She was just pretending, in case the light, scratching knock on the door had been Natalie back again. 'Have a listen to this.'

'What?'

Anna squinted up at Chris, pushing her hair out of her eyes, and reluctantly accepted the personal stereo. She put on the headset.

'What have you given me this for?' She shouted over music only she could hear. 'You know I hate this kind of thing!'

'Forward it a bit,' Chris shouted back, 'but keep listening.'

Anna hit fast forward and then stopped. She listened, her frown deepening. She rewound and listened intently, her dark eyes widening and her mouth twitching at the corners. She rewound the tape and listened a third time. Chris watched, hugging herself. She was shivering, although it was not cold.

'Wow!' Anna said as she stopped the tape. 'You've got to hand it to him – he's got nerve. When did you get this?'

'Just now. That knock on the door was Mark and Dave, they just handed me the tape. Said I was to listen to it on my personal stereo, and that they'd be back for my answer in the morning – and not to play it to anybody else.'

'Well, you've certainly been careful to follow their instructions so far, Chris. Here you are.' Anna handed it back.

'What do you think?'

Chris accepted the tape machine without saying anything. She didn't know what to think. She had not known what to expect, but certainly not this. She could hardly believe it. It was kind of flattering, but somehow shocking as well.

'Let's have another listen,' Anna said.

They held the headset between them. Chris fumbled the controls so Anna found the right stretch of tape. There was a loud click and white noise and then Andy's voice interrupted the music:

Hi, Chris! Guess who? It's me – Andy – Andy Henderson. Look – I know we don't know each other very well – but I really like you – and I wondered if you . . . you would go out with me?

There were clicks and a space and some muttered swearing and then the voice came back.

Er . . . I hope you decide it's 'yes' because I really do find you interesting and I like you a whole lot. Please say 'yes' – you won't regret it, and, believe me, it wouldn't just be a short-term thing. Yes or no – give me your answer in the morning. I'll be waiting to hear from you. Er, that's all. Andy.

The music crashed back. Anna could no longer control her silent shaking laughter. Chris took the machine from her and stopped the tape.

'I'm sorry, Chris,' Anna said eventually. 'It's just that he sounds such a dick head. *I really do find you interesting!*' She snorted with laughter. 'No wonder he didn't want anyone else to hear it! What on earth are you going to say?'

'I don't know. I'll have to think about it. I mean, he doesn't even know me. But I don't think it's right to laugh at it. OK?'

'All right, I'm sorry.' Anna cleared her throat and put on a serious face. 'Maybe he knows you better than you think.'

'What do you mean?'

Anna lit a cigarette. 'He fancies you, that much is obvious. Maybe,' she inhaled and rested her chin on her hand, 'maybe he's been watching you for a while. Like he hardly took his eyes off you in Dave's room just now – and at the service station and on the bus this morning. Maybe he's been there all the time and you just haven't been aware of him.'

'How can he say he likes me? He doesn't even know me.'

'Oh, come on, Chris! Don't be so naïve. Perhaps he likes what he sees! You ought to be flattered.'

Chris flushed slightly and looked away. 'I know. I am flattered. What do you think I ought to do?'

Anna considered the tape for a moment, turning it over in her hand.

'Well,' she said at last, 'he's the last person I'd figure to do something like that.' She shrugged. 'Maybe I've misjudged him. It's kind of sweet that he'd make such a prat of himself to ask you out. Now open the window so we can get rid of this smoke. There's no need to make a big deal out of it, he's not proposing. Why not? You're not going out with anyone at the moment. It could be fun.' She stretched and yawned. 'What have you got to lose?'

'I don't know. What about . . .'

Anna was alerted by the dreamy secret smile, she knew

what was coming. This was going to be difficult. She decided the only thing to do was take a deep breath and tell her.

'Look, Chris. I wouldn't worry too much about Nick.' Anna's voice changed from joking, so did her face. 'After the disco, he took you home, right?'

'Yeah? So?'

'Well, after he'd taken you home, he came back for Diane and . . .'

'And?'

'And he went with her.'

The words came out in a rush. Chris felt as though a dental anaesthetic was freezing her face, preserving her silly expression, guaranteeing any words that she said would come out lumpy and blurred. They didn't, they just sounded as though they were being spoken by a little girl.

'What do you mean? Went with her? Where did they go?'

'I don't know where they went, Chris. What does it matter where they went?' Anna's dark eyes flared with impatience but it wasn't Chris who was making her angry. 'All I know is he met her outside Bridge Parade chip shop and she went with him. You know what I mean!'

'Why?'

'How do I know?' Anna couldn't look at Chris's puzzled, hurt expression. 'Because she would. Because he could. You know what a slag she is.'

'How do you know? How do you know all this?'

'I know because I was there.' Anna sighed. 'I saw them. He came up, grinning all over his face. They chatted. They went off together.'

'Why didn't you tell me?'

'I didn't know how you'd react. Didn't know how serious you were about him.' Anna looked away.

'Thought maybe you wouldn't find out, then it wouldn't matter.'

'So why are you telling me now?'

'Because you've got a chance to go out with someone else. It wouldn't be right for me to let you pass it up because of Nick. He's just not worth it.'

'I suppose everyone knows,' Chris said miserably.

'Well, there were a fair few there. I mean, she wasn't outside the chippy on her own.'

Chris thought about the Disco. How proud she'd been, how glad that they'd been seen by everyone.

'Makes me look a real . . .'

But she couldn't finish the sentence. Her smile was fractured, sick and sad.

'No, it doesn't.' Anna hugged her. 'It makes him look like a shit and her look like a slag, but it doesn't make you look like anything. All I'm saying is forget him. If he'd do a trick like that he's not worth bothering with. Make your own mind up about going out with Andy and just leave Nick out of it. Now come on.' She pulled Chris close for a second and then let her go. 'Let's get some sleep. And close the window, will you. It's freezing.'

Chris turned out the light and walked over to the window. As she reached out to close it she saw headlights up on the bend in the road. She stood for a moment, listening for but not hearing the car driving past. Chris wanted to call Anna over but she was already buried under her duvet. She turned from the window and went back to bed, trying to shake off the feeling that there had been eyes watching behind the twin points of light as they blinked out.

Anna's light breathing acted like a regulator on her thinking and she found her mind drifting back to Nick and Diane. They walked in her dreams, arms round each

34

other, laughing and talking, kissing under a street lamp before turning away from her, into the darkness of the park.

When she had first played Andy's tape, she had no idea what she was going to say to him. In the morning she had no trouble making her mind up, no trouble at all.

Chapter 7

He doused the car's headlights and cut the engine, letting it roll silently down the hill until he had a clear view of the house. It had been a good idea, taking a car. Got him here in no time. He wondered why he hadn't thought of it before.

He'd had a couple of drinks. It had been a bit of a risk but he was glad he'd taken it. The locals, playing pool and the fruit machine in the small country pub, took no notice of him. He had read the notices about darts contests and fishing competitions and stared at the empty fag packets in the grate. No one bothered him and when he'd had enough he went out to the car park and helped himself to a car. Sometimes you need a few drinks. It helped you think, gave you courage to do things, to take risks that you wouldn't normally take.

He'd had a couple of drinks on Friday or he would not have had the guts to do it. On his way home he'd taken a short cut across the graveyard, and she was there. He suddenly knew he could not bear to go back to his room, where he thought about her and dreamt about her and said the words that must be said, but only to himself, only inside his head. He had stood wondering what to do, while street lights flicked on red through the dark canopies of the trees and white marble monuments gave back light stored up in the day. Cellophane gleamed on the mound of a freshly dug grave.

She was coming past the church, taking a short cut just like him. She did not notice him until she was quite near. She flicked her hair out of her eyes, tucking it back behind her ear. He was close now, as close as he had ever been, memorizing every movement, every tiny detail, so he would be able to play it back later in his head.

She kind of jerked when she saw him, not a nice movement. Fine hairs rose like fur on her arm. Their eyes met. She knew him. She had seen him before. She remembered his pale eyes, colourless as tap water. There had been an accident. Every head in the street had turned towards the bang, the breaking of glass and rending of metal, every head except his. He had been looking the other way entirely, staring straight at her. Her house key imprinted its pattern on to the hand in her pocket as she stepped away from the side of the church, away from him.

He felt the smile freeze on his face and the gladness freeze in his heart. She was walking away. He felt stupid then, standing there with his mouth half open, framed for the words he had been aching for so long to say. He only wanted to speak to her. That was all. Just a few words to tell her how he loved her. And she was walking away from him. In a couple of yards she would be out of the wooden gates and into the street and he would have lost his chance.

Fear hit her like a punch in the throat. Her eyes blurred, she could hardly see to walk. But she did not run. To run would be to admit that this was happening. Her body seemed to be working in slow motion, like in a dream. The weight of his hand on her shoulder became inevitable.

He didn't know how long he had been sitting there, but when he came back to where he was, the cold had crept right through him. He grabbed a jacket from the back seat, pulling it close around him. Nights were still cold this time of year, however hot it was in the day, and the old scars on his wrists and at the base of his hands throbbed and ached.

He made no sound as he got out of the car. The house looked deserted, no lights anywhere, but he knew they were in there. It was too dark to make out the markings on the sides of the minibuses parked in the driveway but they probably belonged to some kind of school. It didn't matter who these people were or why they had come; they were in his place, taking up his space, making it impossible for him to do what he'd come here for.

He stood on the edge of the overhang, staring down. It was simple, really. Very simple. He'd make sure they wouldn't want to stay here any more.

Chapter 8

Chris was late for breakfast. She had hung round in the room, making excuses to herself, and now a few burnt and ruptured sausages, a couple of limp strands of bacon and dried-up beans were all that were left.

She grabbed a mug of coffee and sat down. No one looked at her which meant that they all knew. Andy and his mates were over in the corner, finishing off. It was obvious where most of the food had gone. On the table in front of her a few cornflakes floated in a puddle of milk. She was glad that breakfast was not her favourite meal. She wondered when they would make their move.

'Er . . .' Someone cleared his throat behind her. 'Can we see you outside . . .?'

This was what she had been waiting for but Dave's voice still made her jump.

'Sure.' She didn't look at him. 'I'll just finish my coffee.'

'OK. Come on, Mark.'

They went out and Chris stared after them. Then she slowly got out of her chair and followed them. Andy did not even glance up as she left the room.

Anna sat on the bus, consumed by impatience. Where the hell was Peters? Day 1: Sea/Coastal Activities was his show. They were supposed to be spending the morning sea-water canoeing. They would be doing it in the dark at this rate. That would be a shame. An ironic grin flitted across Anna's face, because then they wouldn't get the full effect of the wet suit she was planning to wear. There was no sign of Steadman or Peters, just Chris talking to some bloke who had arrived a few minutes ago in a car. She pointed towards the house and the guy thanked her. Anna moved her legs to make room as Chris came up the aisle.

'I'm going to be sitting at the back with Andy,' Chris said, blushing slightly.

'Suit yourself.' Anna didn't bother hiding her annoyance. 'Where is everybody? Who was that guy you were talking to?'

'I don't know.' Chris shrugged. 'Says he's a policeman. Wants to talk to whoever's in charge. See you, Anna.'

'Yeah. See you,' Anna muttered, turning away.

'Anyone sitting there?' Gary leered down at the seat next to her.

'No.'

'Can I sit there?'

'No.'

Gary draped himself along the back of the seat in front of Anna and gestured out of the window. 'Who's that guy?' he said.

'How should I know? Chris says he's a policeman.'

'D'you reckon? Looks like he slept in that jacket. Could be anybody.'

Anna followed his gaze. The man was talking to Ms Steadman now. He was slightly smaller than her, casually dressed with scruffy dark hair and very pale. She shrugged. That was the point, wasn't it? Plain-clothes policemen were supposed to look like anybody. Steadman stood listening, massaging her forehead. The man kicked at the slaty ground and stuck his hands deeper in his pockets. You could tell that whatever he was telling her was pretty heavy.

'Looks even less like a copper than the last one did and if he's flashed any ID, I haven't seen it.'

'So what?' Anna snarled up at him. 'What are you telling me for? Go to the back and talk to Chris if you're so interested and leave me alone.'

The car roared off and Anna stretched her legs out. There was more space now Chris was sitting with Andy but it was going to be really boring. Steadman had gone to meet Peters when he finally came out, shouting something about security, and then they'd both gone back into the house. Anna groaned to herself. Her whole body felt tense and wound up. When were they going to get on with what they had come here for? Why didn't they come and start the bus?

It had the feel, smell and texture of an old walrus skin. The ancient pimply rubber had faded to grey, and white stress marks showed like thread veins. The parts that got the most friction had given up altogether and Chris could see her white thighs through the frayed holes. Bits of spongy pale-blue lining poked out. She picked off a lump of rubber and flicked it away.

'This suit's disgusting,' she said to Michaela, the next one to emerge from the bus. 'And I was looking forward to this bit!'

'Christ, look at mine then!' Michaela pulled at her wet suit. 'The crutch is round my knees and the zipper doesn't work properly.'

Michaela waddled over to Chris and eased herself down on to a log.

'Doesn't even bend in the right places,' she said.

Chris laughed. 'Think of all the bodies that have been crammed into these.'

'Urr . . . yeah . . .' Michaela giggled and grimaced, 'boys and all. I'm glad the crutch is round my knees.'

'Funny colour,' Diane said as she emerged from the bus. 'Hey! Why isn't mine black like yours?'

'Because you've got yours on inside out,' Chris said when she could speak again. 'Rubber's outside.'

'Oh, shit.' Diane looked inside the suit. 'How was I to know? It's the smallest one there and all. Only just got my tits in it.' Her voice was whining up into panic. 'I'll never get out of it now!'

Her panic was justified. The rubber had moulded around her like a vacuum pack. It was taking a great deal of pulling and hauling to shift it at all.

'Watch it! You're taking me bikini bottom with it!'

'Don't make such a fuss, Diane,' Chris grunted. She was sweating now. 'Nobody can see you. That's it!'

Chris and Michaela had one leg each and, in one last great effort, they managed to pull the suit down. Diana made a grab for the bikini bottom and missed. Appreciative cheering broke out from the dune behind them. Diane let out a high screeched wail and made a run for it, but her feet were effectively tied at the ankles by the rumpled suit and she sprawled headlong in the sand and scrubby grass. The cheering changed to delighted laughter.

'Don't just stand there. Help me up!' Tears of rage and humiliation were streaking mascara down Diane's face.

Chris threw her a towel and the laughter turned to whistles and boos. Shouts of, '*More, More, More! Off, Off, Off!*' thickened into chanting as the three girls made it in tight formation back to the bus.

Michaela pushed Diane up the steps to sort her out and calm her down. Chris sat down and waited. It couldn't have happened to a better person, really. She didn't feel so bad about Diane now.

Natalie waddled up. 'What's happening? Anything I can do?'

'No, it's all over. You missed the show. Diane put her wet suit on inside out.' Chris regarded the other girl critically. 'Christ, Nat – you sure you've got yours on right? Thought mine was short in the leg but you look like a chimp. Sure you haven't put your legs down the arm holes?'

'Even if she has we haven't got time to sort it out now,' interrupted Ms Steadman. She shouted up into the bus, 'Will you lot stop messing about and get your acts together? Come on the rest of you and follow me!'

'Why isn't her suit like ours?' Natalie asked Chris as they trailed along after her like a troop of penguins.

'Because it's her own. It hasn't been worn by generations of school kids.'

'I hope I've got a figure like that when I'm her age.'

'You've got to be joking, Nat,' Diane said as she caught up with them, 'you're never going to have a figure like that!' Diane seemed to have recovered from her ordeal.

'Anna,' Ms Steadman shouted over to the group standing by the stacked canoes, 'come over here and sort out this lot, will you?'

Diane nudged Michaela. 'Christ, look at her! What a poser! Why are we the only ones with the crap suits?'

'It belongs to her stepbrother, Paul.' Chris watched Anna saunter over. She looked like she'd stepped out of a travel feature in *Elle*. 'He does a lot of wind surfing. What's so funny?'

Anna grinned at them. 'Nothing. Glad I caught your

43

act, Di. What do you do for an encore?' At Diane's muttered reply, her grin widened. 'Nah, you'd be better at that than me, you've had more practice. Come on – grab one of these.'

She hauled a canoe on to her shoulder and started off towards the beach.

The rest of them clunked along behind her. By the time they got down to the beach, Anna was already a long way out, cutting through the heavy surf to where the other group were riding the big waves. Ms Steadman had told them to stay well in-shore, but she didn't need to worry, they had no intention of venturing out there. Their plan was to get out and start sunbathing as soon as possible.

They couldn't even make it past the shallow water. Every wave beached them. Diane was the first to give up.

'Sod this for a lark,' she said as she hauled her canoe out of the water. 'I'm not exactly the outdoor type, know what I mean?'

Chris and Michaela followed.

'Coming, Natalie?' Chris shouted.

Natalie looked at the dots out to sea for a moment and then swallowed her doubts. They were letting her go with them. She couldn't believe her luck.

'Got any fags?'

Michaela shook wet hair out of her eyes. 'Does it look like it?' she said, pulling at her glistening suit.

'I'm going back to get some then.' Diane turned away. 'Find you later.'

They watched her make her way back down the beach and then headed for the dunes.

'Won't the van be locked?' Natalie asked as she puffed along beside them.

Michaela stopped and looked at her. 'Maybe,' she shrugged. 'Doesn't matter if it is. Di can get into anything. Her brother showed her.'

They started off again and Natalie stumbled on. The soft white sand made it hard going but she did not want to be left behind.

They disappeared over the crest of the dune without looking back, so they didn't see Mark, down the other end of the beach, coming in like a train. Two small rivers met here and flowed out into the sea across miniature deltas of flat stones, their waters swirling past lines of sharp black rocks that were only just now breaking the surface. Steadman had told them to keep away from here, but what did she know?

The outgoing tide had brought the surf up. Mark had caught the wave way out, judging it just right. This one would take him all the way. He could feel the wicked power beneath him, not like in the school swimming-pool. That was rubbish – this was what he'd come for. This was the business. The wave, hard and glassy, seemed to have the whole of the Irish sea behind it. He felt its huge force surging under him, coursing through his whole body until he was part of it, but he was riding it, controlling the wave. The canoe cut through the water like a power boat. He was grinning like a kid. He couldn't help it, tasting the sea in the salty spray. This was the best, the best ever. There were no words to describe this sensation, the feeling of exultation it gave.

The hypnotic razor hiss turned into growing thunder. He twisted to see what was behind, seconds stretched and he seemed to have time to stare right into the base of the green cliff of water towering over him. The canoe slewed side on and it felt like the whole ocean was falling on top

45

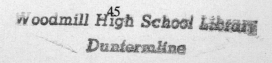

of him as the wave broke in a boiling mass of surf and foam.

'You going with him, or what?' Michaela asked as she stripped off her wet suit.

Chris chewed on a stem of marram grass and did not reply. Chris liked Michaela well enough. For a time, years back, they had been quite close friends, in the Juniors and when they first went to the Comprehensive. Then Chris had met Anna and she and Michaela had drifted apart. Michaela had been as chubby as Natalie then and almost as plain. Chris could remember her freckled round face split by a grin full of braces, her mousy hair always pulled back tight into a pony tail or bunches, stretching all the skin across her forehead. There was not much left of that little girl now. Unlike Natalie, Michaela had developed in all the right places and she had learnt to make the best of what she had got. Her hair was bleached and permed in the shop where she worked on Saturdays. Her ambition was to be a stylist and beauty consultant and she already had a job lined up.

'Well, are you, or what?' Michaela asked again.

Chris didn't want to talk about this. The idea of Andy and herself as a couple made her feel strange. She needed time to get used to it. It was too new to discuss with anyone, she hadn't even talked to Anna about it, let alone Michaela. Whatever she told Michaela would be reported straight back to Diane.

'You're a bit of a dark horse, aren't you? He's really nice. Loads fancy him.' Michaela lay back in the sand and allowed her eyes to go dreamy. 'If it was me, I'd be dead chuffed. I'm telling you, Di's well sick,' she laughed, 'sick as a parrot.'

'Why should she feel sick about it?'

'Are you kidding? God. She's been mad on him for ages.' Michaela glanced over at Natalie and lowered her voice. 'That's why . . .'

Natalie sat by herself, humming. She knew they didn't want her here. No one shared this sort of talk with her. They huddled together, laughing, talking and smiling, but as soon as she came near the warmth left their eyes and was replaced by blank stares or hostility. Chris's blue-green eyes were friendly enough but Michaela was not bothering to hide how she felt. Natalie endured that look every day.

'Think I'll go for a walk,' she said.

'I mean, she's not . . .' Michaela broke off what she was going to say. 'Good idea, see you.'

'You sure, Natalie?' Chris looked up at her. 'Don't feel you have to.'

'No, Chris, it's all right.' A smile lit up Natalie's homely face. 'Need to stretch my legs. I like the seaside, anyway.'

The other two girls watched her scramble away and then rolled back to their former positions.

'I heard she wasn't interested,' Chris said after a while. 'That she fancied someone else.'

'Yeah, well,' Michaela grinned, 'who doesn't she fancy? But Andy's different. She's been nuts on him for ages but he hasn't looked at her since he started getting serious about that Elaine. That's why she's here. I'm doing this as an Option, right? Ever since I got chucked off Typing. Di came because she reckoned she had a chance of getting off with him. She's not exactly the Outdoor Pursuits type, is she?' Michaela's laugh was high and neighing. 'More the Indoor Pursuits type, know what I mean?'

Michaela looked over for some response but got

nothing. Chris just sat there, making patterns in the sand, chewing on a bit of marram grass.

'Well, are you or not?' she finally asked. Chris was deliberately making this hard work.

Chris shrugged and grinned. 'He asked me and I said yes so I suppose that means I am going out with him.'

Chris rolled on to her back and closed her eyes, stretching out under the warm sun. Conversation over, Michaela thought, as she pushed her hands deep in the fine white sand. But now, at least, we know.

The big wave had turned Mark over and the one behind and the one behind that were making sure he stayed that way. The canoe was being tumbled in the waves like a toy. Mark had tried again and again to right himself, but in the school swimming-pool there was nothing that kept pushing him back like this. And something had happened to the apron, his legs were pinned. Panic began to rise through him, forcing the air he had left out of his lungs. He was stuck. He could not get out. He could feel bubbles leaking out of his nose and from the corner of his mouth. He could see nothing. Sea-water stung and blinded him and filled his throat with a thick salt taste that made him want to retch. It was not like the swimming-pool. He was drifting and drifting in the bright blue water, looking up through the ripples that broke up the light. His head filled with bright changing patterns, forming and re-forming in fluid combination. They began to pulse and flash and then exploded into black. His hands let go of the sides of the canoe and air bubbles streamed out of him, joining the foaming surf above his head.

*

Anna had paddled back to check on Chris and Di but there was no sign of them, just their canoes dragged up on the beach. They're probably in the dunes or the cafe, she thought, as she navigated a wave, and turned back out to sea. Suddenly she saw Mark, coming in on a big wave, way down the beach. There was no one else around so she headed over to join him but, when she looked again, he wasn't there. She scanned the beach, he wasn't there either. He should have come up by now if he was still in the water. She saw a flash of bright orange in the pounding surf near the shore line and doubled her speed.

There was no one else around. She was his only chance and she couldn't afford to make any mistakes. If she didn't manage it first time they could both be dragged back and forth until the sea threw them up on the beach, or smashed them on to the black smooth rocks that gaped like a mouth a few metres away. She had located him now, or at least his canoe belly up in the water, and she struggled to hold her position against the constant tug and pull of the waves. When she saw the wave reach under to curl him up again, she dug in and ploughed down with all her force. She caught under the lead edge of the big canoe and used the power of the outgoing tide to turn him up. One look told her that he was in no position to help himself. She grappled and held on and prayed for the next wave to take them in.

He was desperately heavy and the vicious undertow dragged the sand and stones from under her feet, dumping her back in the water and losing the precious few feet that she had gained. She held his head on her chest, trying to keep it out of the water. His skin was blotched grey and livid purple, his lips putty coloured and tinged with blue. She searched desperately up and down the deserted beach. They weren't going to make it. The tears on her face were warm but tasted of the sea. In the distance she saw a lonely little figure like a comma. She used what strength she had left and yelled.

Natalie thought it was the screaming of the gulls at first. Then she realized, and ran.

'Grab his other arm.' Anna's words rasped above the crashing waves, her breathing was harsh and laboured. 'We've got to get him further up the beach.'

They dragged the heavy length of him between them, his feet making deep furrows in the sand.

'Something's going on down there.'

Diane stood on the crest of the dune, outlined against the sky, shading her eyes and squinting down the beach.

'Hey get out of the sun, Di,' Chris shivered. 'You're casting a bloody great shadow and making it cold.'

Michaela hugged her arms about her. 'I don't like it here no more. I've got a funny feeling – like we're being watched.'

'Oh, don't be so stupid!' Chris said, but she'd felt it too. She wrapped a towel round her and started to get up.

'Shut it you two!' Diane shouted. 'There's something serious going on down there. I'm going to take a look.'

They knew it was Anna by the panels on her suit and Natalie by her shape, but they could not tell who lay on the sand between them. Anna was kneeling over whoever it was and appeared to be passionately kissing them, pausing every few seconds to come up for air. As they got nearer, Chris thought it might be Mark.

'He'll be all right. He'll be all right. She knows what she's doing. He'll be all right.'

The words set themselves to the rhythm of her running and flattened into a chant. Just as they got there Mark

50

twitched, rolled over sideways, and spewed sea-water all over Anna's knees.

They were so busy that none of them noticed, high up on the cliff behind them, the sun glinting on glass and a car turning away from the sea.

Chapter 9

Chris was glad to be out and doing something. They had been given some free time in a small seaside town further up the coast, as soon as they got there everyone had piled into the nearest cafe and looked set to stay there for the rest of the afternoon.

Andy held her arm to steady her, as they stumbled across the fat worms of cables towards the small fairground, and didn't let go. She didn't mind. If they were supposed to be going out with each other, they might as well get on with it, without an audience. She wanted to be alone with him now, away from all the watching eyes. In the cafe there had been Natalie's little rodent beads, staring over the rim of her thick shake, full of candid curiosity, Diane nervously fidgeting with a cherry Coke, giving them the once over when she thought they weren't looking and Anna's steady dark stare, full of brooding speculation. And that was just the front row. There was another kind of interest from all his nudging and leering mates. It was like being on *Blind Date*. She had been grateful to Andy for noticing and suggesting that they tried out the fair.

'What do you want to go on first?' he asked.

He had to shout. Screaming and music, flaring and duelling from each ride, surrounded them. Chris sucked in the sharp blue diesel and sweet candy floss smell and grinned at him.

52

'The waltzers, let's go on the waltzers first. I love the waltzers!'

He grinned back at her and squeezed her hand. 'Yeah, I like them too, the waltzers are the only ride.'

He darted through the waiting, jostling crowd and leapt between the still circling cars. He moved with the same assurance and deft grace as the boys who worked the fair. He jumped one of the cars as a couple stumbled out and stood, strong legs braced against the safety bar, beckoning her over.

'Here, mate,' he said, handing the fairground boy a five pound note. 'Give us as long as this buys.'

Chris was thrilled. Usually she had to wait ages with whoever she was with to even get on and then they only had one mingy go. When the movement of the car threw her against him, she did not move away.

Afterwards he handed her the hot dog he had bought her and said, 'Christ, you're something else!'

He was laughing at her, but there was a respect in his eyes that she could get to look for, get to want. He kicked at a stone, flicking it up and bouncing it on the toe of his trainer.

'Most girls I know would have thrown up,' he laughed. 'Most *guys* I know would have thrown up!'

'Not me,' she mumbled through the extra onions, 'I love it!'

'So do I.' He wiped some sauce off her chin. 'Finally found a girl who likes fairs as much as I do. What are we waiting for? Let's do it!'

He grabbed her hand and dragged her off towards the dodgems. She had never been to the fair with someone like him. He was absolutely in command, breezing them on and off rides, in and out of the waiting, jittering crowds. They never had to wait, slumped in disappointment and doubt, keying themselves up for the next time around. She didn't know how he did it but it made her feel proud and glad to be with him. And he won things, at darts, shooting – anything; he never missed. Big prizes too. The last boy she had been to the fair with had only managed to get a furry banana and that was on hook-a-duck. She could hardly carry all the stuff Andy had won for her. Everything went right. It was like being with a boy in a film, and so far it hadn't cost her anything.

'Put it back in your pocket,' he had said. 'You're with me. If you're with me, you don't pay. I've got plenty, I pay for everything.'

'One thing left and then we've done the lot.' He stood, hands in pockets, gazing up at the slowly turning wheel. 'Let's go.'

He gave the coconut he was carrying under his arm to an old lady and her grandson and strode off towards the little booth under the Big Wheel. Chris followed reluctantly. She hated the Big Wheel. She did not even like to get this close to it. She did not like to see the thin taut wires and rusty meccano struts that held it up.

'No! Andy wait! I don't like the Big Wheel!'

'I don't like to leave until I've been on everything,' he said. 'It's kind of a personal thing with me. A challenge, you know?'

He handed the money to the man in the booth. He did not seem to hear her fear and reluctance.

'Here we are – quick!' He dragged her with him and up into the next yawning car as it swung down.'You'll be all right with me.'

He put his arm around her as the safety bar snicked shut, and held her as the boy gave the car a push. She wondered if it would be as bad this time, if having him there would make a difference. The car clicked up and up as couple after couple joined the wheel. They got to the top. The car creaked gently to and fro and she tried to ignore the slight sideways movement of the whole wheel in the wind. His hand was warm, sliding down inside her shirt and caging her breast. She sat completely still and stared straight out at the horizon, trying to work out where the sky met the sea.

Anna moved up a bit as Ms Steadman came and sat next to her. She was asking where everybody was. It was a fair enough question, as there was only Mark, Natalie and herself there and it should have been everybody, but Anna didn't feel like talking so she just shrugged and looked away.

It wasn't Ms Steadman. She didn't mind Ms Steadman. She was OK for a teacher and she wasn't boring, not like the rest of the stiffs. She taught English most of the time and did Outdoor Pursuits because she liked it, because that's what she wanted to do. And she was good. She devoted time to it, went climbing in the holidays when Peters was probably stuck at home grouting the tiles in his bathroom. She knew that Doug Scott bloke who came to the school to do a talk every year. She climbed with strength and grace and ice-cool confidence. Anna had learnt a lot from her. And she loved it, you could tell. She found it exciting; the physicality and danger and risk turned her on. Anna had seen it in her eyes and straight away recognized it, because that's how she felt.

The teacher leaned forward, her long brown arms resting on the edge of the table, and tried again.

'I said six o'clock and there's hardly anybody here. Where are all the rest?'

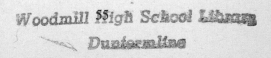

'Can I get you anything, Miss?' Mark said, getting up and indicating the counter.

She looked over at the espresso machine, piles of cheese sandwiches and pyramids of Coke cans and dug in her pocket for change.

'I'll get these. Same again?' Anna and Natalie nodded. Mark stood waiting. 'What will it be then, Miss?'

'Oh, sorry, Mark.' She looked up at him, pushing her thick dark hair out of her eyes. Her smile was sudden and brilliant, softening and transforming the taut tense lines of her face, making her look much younger. Mark's colour deepened. 'Coffee would be fine, thanks. Make it black.'

'Is he OK?' she asked as he made his way towards the counter. 'It's just that earlier, I didn't think he looked too good. He was as pale as death.'

Anna shrugged again.

'As far as I know,' she said, and shot a warning glance at Natalie.

They had all been sworn to secrecy. Not because Mark had disobeyed Steadman's orders – he didn't give a toss about that. It was because he didn't want to be shown up in front of his mates. Not all of them. It was Hendy he was worried about. He was supposed to be his best mate but if he found out, Mark would never hear the end of it. He would mock endlessly about something like that: letting himself get turned over by some tiny little wave, having to be rescued by a girl. Anna liked Mark. Underneath his 'hard man' act he was kind-hearted and generous. He deserved better than that. She didn't know what it was about Andy Henderson that made people like Mark want to impress him, made them scared of what he might say, what he might think, what he might do. Mark was so much bigger, so much more powerful. If he wanted he could break Andy in two. Even Chris. Ever since she got that stupid bloody tape message, she'd been as bad as the rest of them. Falling all over him, trotting around after him like a pet dog.

The teacher's steady quizzical stare was still on them, Natalie looked just about to spill her guts. Anna picked up the newspaper that Ms Steadman had thrown on the table when she came in.

'Can I have a look at your paper?' she said. 'Seen this, Nat? You like murders and things.'

Natalie took the garish tabloid from her and mouthed the headlines to herself.

'Bloke must have been a nutter to do this,' she said after a moment. 'What do you think, Miss?'

She turned the front page for them to see and they took in the brutal headlines and the smiling face of a young girl. The girl's prettiness showed despite the blurring of the newspaper photograph. It looked like one of those school portraits, the sort with little brown borders, that pile up on Gran's sideboard, charting the changes in a kid's life year by year. Except there wouldn't be any more of these. This kid's life was over.

'Yes, Natalie.' Ms Steadman cleared her throat. 'He must be.'

'That's horrible! Have you read it?' Natalie chewed at a fingernail. 'All those weddings going on and nobody knowing a thing. That'll mean bad luck.'

'Let's have a look.' Anna held out her hand for the paper.

Natalie turned back to Ms Steadman. Her brow suddenly furrowed with thick lines of apprehension as she said, 'Miss? You don't think it could be him, do you? You know – the one that policeman was talking about, the one they're looking for?'

'What do you know about that, Natalie?' The teacher's

57

reply was cool and guarded, but her look was as sharp as steel.

'Oh, I – er – dunno.' Natalie started to colour. 'Just something I heard someone say, that's all.'

'Here you go, Miss,' Mark grinned down at her and handed her a Polystyrene cup. 'Come on, Anna. Shift up.'

'Everyone's gone to the fair,' Natalie said, taking advantage of Mark's return to change the subject. 'Except us. We weren't bothered.'

'What about you, Anna?' Ms Steadman blew on her coffee. 'Where's Chris?'

Anna opened her mouth to reply-but Natalie provided the words.

'She doesn't like fairs, Miss. And Chris has gone with Andy Henderson.'

'Do you know everything or what?' Anna glared at Natalie. 'Have you got a little computer in your head that tells you what everyone is doing and where they are and what they are thinking at any given time?'

'No.' Natalie put on her wounded puppy look. 'I just watch people and listen to what they say, that's all.'

'Well,' Anna's full mouth turned down into a sulk, 'you can stop watching me and listening to my conversations. All right?'

Natalie shrugged and drooped.

'Lay off, Anna.' Mark put down the sugar pourer and touched her arm. 'Nat didn't mean anything. It's not her fault.'

Liz Steadman sighed and swilled her coffee round. What was going on here? Anna sitting next to Mark Gordon, Chris off with Andrew Henderson. Was that enough to account for all the tension that seemed to be about?

'Come on,' she said. 'We'll have to go and round them up. I told Mr Peters six-thirty.'

The early evening crowds were coming out now. Natalie made her way between them, reading the paper she had reclaimed from Anna, bumping into things and people. Liz Steadman waited for her at the corner. The fairground lights shone brighter in the fading light and the sound came and went on the wind.

'You forgot this,' Natalie puffed up and handed her the newspaper. 'You know, I reckon it is,' she said as she fell in step beside her.

'You reckon what is?'

'Him,' Natalie said, pointing at the front page of the paper. 'I reckon it's the same fella. The one there and the one they're looking for.'

'It might be, Natalie,' Ms Steadman said. Natalie could not read the expression in the tall teacher's eyes. 'But then again it might not be. One way or the other, we have no proof. In any event I don't want you scaring yourself silly with something that is only idle speculation, or frightening anybody else. Do you understand me?'

'Yes, Miss,' Natalie nodded, trying to work out what she was talking about.

'Good. As long as that's understood. Now come along, we can't stay here all day dawdling. At this rate, we'll never get back.'

'Miss, d'you think . . .'

But Ms Steadman was already half-way down the street. Natalie had to scuttle fast to keep up with her. Ms Steadman did not hear or chose to ignore the rest of her questions and the creased-up newspaper went into the next bin where it settled down among the chip papers and fast-food cartons, used news.

Chapter 10

It wouldn't have happened, he really thought it would not have happened, if she had not struggled. He had only wanted to talk to her, make her understand how he felt about her. He loved her for Christ's sake! He did not want to hurt her. That was the last thing. But he'd had to stop her. There had only been a door between her and a street full of people. He felt again the sweat start out and the tears come into his eyes. Another inch and she'd be away down the street. He could not allow her to go now. The moment she turned round, her eyes huge and black and the street lights on the bones of her face casting shadows, she had known too, known he was someone special. He had to get her away from that door that led out of the churchyard and into somewhere quiet. Somewhere they could be alone together. Somewhere they could talk.

Panic had made him strong. Her hair had felt like scrunched silk in his hands. He had been surprised and a little bit angry that she would want to fight him. The strength of her resistance had made him feel upset. It was not necessary. He touched the half-healed lines her nails had scored down the side of his face and neck and pulled up his collar. It had hurt him inside that she should think that she had to behave that way. Besides it was pointless. He was so much stronger.

He wandered around, seeing but not seeing, the little seaside town. They used to come here on day trips sometimes, to the beach and the fair and shopping, when he was a kid. He had loved those days, special treats. It had been magic then. Spoilt now, of course. He looked around in disgust. Full of big fat tourists, shiny red and peeling, like burns victims. Cooked they looked, like sausages, as if their skin would crack and break and the underneath flesh show through and ooze like that. He itched an eczema sore on his hand. And all these kids running around, screaming and shouting to each other and behaving stupidly. It was making his head ache. Bad.

He had followed them from the house. They had gone to the sea first. It was the place he had always loved best, next to the high hills. He had felt good, driving along the coast past mile after mile of deserted beaches and golden sands. But they had stopped at his favourite place, spewing out of the minibuses, shouting and shrieking like gulls. He had stayed there for a bit watching them through their own binoculars, mucking about, messing up the clean white sand. He had looked forward to visiting these places to find good memories. But all he kept finding were things to upset him, and it was not good for him to be upset. Not good at all.

Angie's face was there in the trash can, looking up from in between paper cups and crisp packets. The headlines told him that they had found her. He had better be careful now, not do anything to attract attention. He was not safe here. He would only be safe in the place that was home, where nothing could hurt him, but while they were in there he couldn't go back. Angry tears twisted and knotted up his throat. Well, he'd been down and told them and they'd better take notice. It was the only indication they were going to get.

'Watch it, mate!'

He thought it was a boy, knocking right into him, but

the hair flicked back and a girl's eyes looked into his, green and blue as the sea.

'I'm sorry,' she said, smiling an apology.

He stared back hard and she nearly dropped all the crap she was carrying: goldfish and stupid furry toys.

'All right, mate?' The boy with her grinned as he pulled her away. 'Come on, Chris.'

He watched them go. She was laughing now, leaning against the boy as he held her arm to guide her through the churning mass of people.

'They're all slags, really,' he thought.

He turned to seek his own amusement in the thickening crowd and chaos of sound and finally found an Arcade. He settled himself into the video games. He could lose himself there, in the black screens, bringing under his control the bright flashes which brought random death and destruction. His fingers whitened, jabbing at the buttons and controls. His mind buzzed with excitement. He played until the screen exploded in a rolling ball of flame that made no sound. GAME OVER flashed up. It was time to leave, time to go home.

Chapter 11

'Where have you been?' Anna said as soon as Chris struggled in through the door. 'What have you done with the fish?'

'Andy and I put them in the pond in the garden,' Chris said, smiling.

'Ooh, how sweet,' Anna lisped sarcastically. 'How was the fair?'

'Great!' Chris grinned happily. 'Andy's brilliant at winning things. Look at all this!'

Anna's stony look over the pile of prizes reminded her of the guy at the fair and she shivered slightly. The recollection of his cold colourless eyes, staring into hers, suddenly clouded her happiness. She frowned, dumping the soft toys she was carrying on to the bed, disturbed by the fact that she'd seen him before, and recently, but couldn't remember where or when.

'They nearly went without you, you know,' Anna said, moodily. 'What made you so late?'

'I was doing something totally out of order called having fun.' Chris sighed. 'Come on, Anna, Why are you being like this?'

'I'm not being like anything.' Anna looked round the room critically. 'You could open a stall of your own,' she said, picking up a shapeless soft toy with 'I Heart You' on it's chest. 'God, this is hideous. Where did you get all this stuff?'

'Andy won it for me,' Chris said, her smile returning.

'Whizzo!' Anna dropped the bear as if it was contaminated.

'Hey!' Chris said, picking him up and hugging him to her. 'What's the matter with you, Anna? Why are you acting this way?'

The bright glowy look was fading from Chris's face, her green eyes were dulling with confusion, her mouth turned down and hurt. Anna looked away. How could she explain how she felt? She could not even explain it to herself.

Anna said nothing. Gradually the glow Chris's face had held, when she spoke about Andy, returned.

'Andy's nice, you know? I really like him. He's dead easy to be with. I mean,' she groped for the words that would explain him to her friend, make her like him too. 'He's easy to talk to. You don't have to worry what you're going to say all the time. And . . .' she fondled the ear of the furry bear, 'he's not boring. Being with him wasn't like being with other boys. He made me feel special. It was exciting. He makes me laugh. It's funny, but I feel I've known him for ages. It all feels so right, so natural.' She stopped for a moment to think some more. 'It's like I'm allowed to be myself when I'm with him. I don't have to pose or put on an act. I can relax, like when I'm with you. He's not at all like I thought.'

Anna lay on the bed and closed her eyes.

'I don't know why you don't like him, Anna. I mean you don't even know him.' Chris regarded the other girl sharply. 'You're not jealous, are you?'

'Jealous? God no.' Anna did not open her eyes. She was not jealous, at least not in the way she took Chris to mean. And it was true she did not know him, although she'd seen him around enough, in school and out, to know what she'd seen of him she did not particularly like.

64

He was very possessive, he never let Elaine out of his sight. There was something about him that reminded her of Paul, her stepbrother. But then Chris didn't know about that. 'Has he asked you to go out with him when we get back?'

'Well, not exactly.'

Despite herself, Chris could feel her face growing hot.

'And if he does?' Anna said, sitting up. 'Will you?'

'I don't know.' Chris turned away and replaced the bear in the middle of her pillow. 'Yes, probably.'

'Oh, yeah?' Anna's voice was harsh with disgust. 'And what about his girlfriend?'

'Elaine?'

'Yes, what about her? Is he going to dump her?'

'I haven't thought about it.' Chris sounded evasive. 'That's his problem.'

'Well, think about it. It is hers, and maybe yours, too.' Anna propped herself up on her elbows and looked over at her. 'I'm sorry, Chris. I didn't mean to be like this. I just don't want you to get into something you can't handle.'

'Since when? You were all for it last night!'

That was last night. Anna shook her head. She had not thought that it would progress so quickly. The relationship was already starting to change things between her and Chris.

'It's just a feeling I get about him. I don't want you to get hurt, that's all.' Anna pushed her hair back out of her eyes and tried to smile. 'Just ignore me. I'm shattered. All that business with Mark.'

'Yeah, sure. You must be,' Chris said, smiling down at her. 'How about Mark? Is he OK now? I saw you were with him on the bus. You really like him, don't you?'

Anna smiled. 'Yes, I do.'

65

Chris grinned, triumphant. 'I thought you did. He really likes you too, you know?'

'Does he?' Anna stared at her. 'How do you know?'

'He's liked you for ages.' Chris stretched and yawned. 'Andy told me this afternoon.'

Anna's voice was dangerously quiet. 'Oh, did he now?'

'Yeah. Andy said Mark'd really like to go out with you, but he's too scared to ask.'

'What does that mean?' Anna stood up. 'Oh, I see. You're going to do the asking for him, is that it? See what you can fix up? Then we can all go out as a foursome and have a fun time together. That'd be nice wouldn't it?' Anna curled her lip in derision. 'The cosy couple scene. I don't think I'm quite ready for that.'

'You don't see anything, Anna.' Chris was suddenly angry. 'I'm not about to act as his go-between. If he wants to ask you, he can do it himself. But if he likes you and you like him, what's wrong with that?'

'There's nothing wrong with it. Except I like him as a friend, not a boyfriend. I don't happen to need everyone to fall in love with me, or vice versa.'

'And I do, I suppose?'

'Looks like it from where I'm standing.' Anna folded her arms and sneered down at Chris. 'You're walking around like an accident waiting to happen. You might as well stick a great big label on your forehead.'

'Maybe I am. Maybe I'm ready for that sort of relationship. You ever think about that?'

'That sort of relationship! You sound like something out of the letter column in *Just Seventeen*,' Anna's voice slipped from sarcasm to simpering parody. '*Dear Anita, I've just met this great boy called Andy and I really think I'm ready for* that *sort of relationship*. You don't know what you're talking about!'

'Oh, and you do, I suppose!' Chris felt herself being pushed beyond endurance. 'How can you know? How can you know anything about it? Anyone comes anywhere near you and you go straight into deep freeze!'

'Maybe I know more than you think I do. And the rate you're going it won't be long before you find out for yourself exactly what I'm talking about!'

'Yeah, well, maybe you do, Anna, and maybe you don't.' They were standing inches apart, shouting into each other's faces. They'd had rows before but never anything like this. Chris turned away, drained and shaking. Her voice dropped to a whisper. 'But you wouldn't tell me anyway, would you? So there's no way for me to know that. Now, if you'll excuse me I've got a previous appointment. I'll see you around.'

Chris slammed the door behind her, furious. There was no talking to Anna when she was like that, let her stew. She looked up and down the corridor, it was quiet and deserted. The fear that had clouded her mood earlier jolted her again. She quickened her step. She needed music, noise, other people to drive Anna and creepy guys at the fairground out of her head. She wanted to find Andy, then she would not have to think about any of it.

Anna lay on the bed and waited. After the anger abated she knew it would be replaced by wave on wave of misery and guilt. It was all her fault. All day she had tried to fight down her uneasiness about this new relationship. After all, she had encouraged Chris to reply to Andy's taped approach. She hadn't been thinking. It had seemed a laugh then, a bit of a joke. She had not realized how serious he was. She might have known that Andrew

Henderson would never do such a thing lightly. When she had seen how it was growing and magnifying in intensity all she had wanted to do was warn Chris about him, and what had she done? Guaranteed delivery, straight into his arms.

How did she know about it? A bitter smile twisted her face. It had happened in Greece last summer, with her dad and his new wife and her new stepbrother, Paul. He had been like the sunlight on the harbour water and she'd been dazzled by him. He was so exciting and glamorous, so unlike the boys at school. She had fallen hopelessly in love and he had obliged by introducing her to more than wind surfing. It had been like an addiction, like a drug. He'd kept on and on and then they had run such risks, taken such chances, never able to get enough of each other. And her dad and his new wife had just been pleased that the 'two kids', as they put it, had so much in common, got on so well. When she came back and it was all over, she couldn't tell Chris, she couldn't tell anyone. Not because she didn't want to, she just couldn't find the words. There were no words to describe the disgust and hatred she felt. Not for Paul, she had got over that, but for herself for being such a fool. And Chris wanted her to go with Mark. She laughed, sharp and humourless and wiped her face on the sleeve of her sweat shirt. She wasn't ready for that.

She lit a cigarette and opened the window, blowing the smoke out into the night. Somewhere below her an engine started. Peters going to the pub, she thought, bloody typical – none of them were even allowed to go out for a walk. Steadman had been prowling around checking and re-checking the locks on all the doors and windows. No one was to go out, on any account. Police orders, apparently. Everyone had to stay put. It looked nice outside too. It would be good to go out alone, Anna thought, into the cool dark, and there were so many stars. The night sky was never like this at home, permanently fogged by city neon – you couldn't see a thing. It is like Greece, she thought, and turned back into the room.

She went back over the row she'd had with Chris, thinking what to do. Once they had both cooled down, once she had apologized, she tried to convince herself, it would be all right. But she knew it would never be the same again, because now there was Andrew Henderson. She had never liked him and her dislike deepened by the minute. She knew she could never like him. He was too like Paul. He got off on having power over people. He collected them: boys, girls, it didn't matter which. He caught them and held them and didn't let go. She couldn't stand to see Chris on display as his latest acquisition, Number One Exhibit.

And if Chris got serious about him? Anna's intense antipathy would be enough to finish them as friends altogether. The best she could hope for would be a part-time friendship, put on hold until Andy wasn't around or for times when they had nothing planned to do together, and from what she knew of him, that would be almost never. She could not imagine her life without Chris in it.

She threw herself back on the bed and fear and misery welled back to fill the space inside her. She couldn't tell Chris, not ever, about how much it would hurt her to be marginalized like that.

Chapter 12

Eventually Anna was driven out to seek some sort of diversion, staying in the room was only making her more and more depressed. There was hardly anyone around and those she found seemed pretty quiet and jumpy. Steadman's strict curfew, the way she was taking it all so seriously, was certainly making the danger they were supposed to be in more of a reality. The tension in the house had suddenly increased. It was not like the other trips Anna had been on; there was something weird about the whole atmosphere.

She was going back to her room when she bumped into Colin and Natalie.

'Hi, Anna. What are you doing?' Natalie sounded bright and cheery at any rate.

'Nothing,' Anna shrugged and put her hands in her pockets. 'Where is everybody?'

'Down with Dave and Gary. Col and me are invited,' she said proudly, 'if we bring the crisps.'

Colin waved a variety pack of twelve in Anna's direction. 'Coming, Anna?' he said.

'I don't know. Who's there?'

'Oh, the usual,' Natalie replied before Colin could speak. 'Gary and Dave, Mark of course, and Diane and Mick. Oh and Chris is there.' She looked over at Colin and giggled. 'With Andy.'

'Might as well, I guess,' Anna said, trying to sound indifferent.

'Come with us.' Natalie was suddenly solemn and serious. 'You shouldn't be by yourself.'

Music rolled out of the door as it opened along with cigarette smoke and fuggy heat.

'Crisps have arrived,' Dave shouted.

'And Anna! Baby! Come and sit next to your Uncle Gaz!' Gary patted a square of vacant carpet beside him and beckoned her over with the bottle he was holding. 'Come over here and have a drink!'

'I'll have a drink,' Anna said as she sat down beside him. 'But don't call me "Baby".'

'Anything you say, Darlin'.'

Anna moved away from the wall, to avoid Gary's arm snaking round her, and took a swig. The thick sweetish stuff slid down her throat and she made a face. The second swig wasn't so bad though and by the third she began to feel distinctly better. Chris and Andy were over on the bed, in the corner, in the shadows. She was determined not to look at them.

Someone turned down the ghetto blaster to minimum volume. Everyone stopped what they were doing, except for the couple on the bed. Even Gary became quiet by her side. Only Natalie's voice could be heard, in the silence that spread around the room, whispering everybody's fear.

'Honestly, Col,' she was saying, 'I read it in the newspaper, so it's got to be true. And the one who did it' – her voice became more dramatic as she gathered in their attention – 'is the same guy who's coming here.'

'How can you be sure, Nat?' Colin whispered.

'I'm sure,' Natalie nodded emphatically, 'because I read it all really carefully. The details are all there. It all fits. There can be no mistake. What's more I asked Ms Steadman about it and she reckons the same as me!'

'He could be coming right now,' Colin breathed. 'It's like that film, *The Hitchhiker*.'

'No!' Gary shrieked. 'It's like *Nightmare on Elm Street* and Freddy's heading straight for you!'

He sprang across and lunged at Natalie, fingers spread and rigid like daggers, his high-pitched unearthly screeching bouncing off the walls of the small room. Everybody jumped and Natalie wailed in terror, burrowing into Colin.

'For Christ's sake, Gary!' Anna shouted, badly startled.

Gary's screaming turned to laughter.

'Joke! Joke! Just a joke, Anna,' he said, as he ambled back to his place. 'What's the matter with you?' he jeered down at her. 'Scared or something?'

'We're all scared, Gary,' Anna said savagely, her voice shaking. 'If you can't see that you're even more of a moron than I thought you were.' She turned on Natalie. 'And you can stop snivelling into Colin's sweatshirt. You don't know any more than anybody else so stop going on and on about it, winding everyone up, and making it worse.'

The party mood was gone. People shuffled round, making moves to go. Anna looked over to the bed where Chris and Andy lay entwined. She watched her friend's hand travel up and down the striped shirt material on Andy's back. She couldn't see what he was doing, but she could imagine. They seemed oblivious to everything. She didn't want to watch them but she couldn't help herself.

'I don't know why they don't go somewhere more private,' Diane said moodily.

'That's because she's not a slag like you,' Gary smiled at Diane, his eyes like chips of glass under drooping lids.

Dave and some of the others sniggered in agreement. Diane's face remained frozen, impassive.

72

'I'm going,' Anna said as she stood up. 'I've had enough of this. How about you, Di?' Diane shrugged. Anna shook her head. Why didn't she say anything to them? How could she take this shit? 'Well, I'm going now.' Anna went over to the bed and grabbed Chris's foot. 'You coming?'

She ignored Gary laughing behind her.

Chris surfaced as if from deep levels of sleep. Her face was flushed and her hair even more tousled than usual. She pulled her shirt down as Andy rolled off her. He lay with his hands behind his head, looking up at Anna. She hoped that bulge in his jeans was giving him pain.

'Yeah . . . er . . .' Chris's voice was husky and thick. Andy leant over her, whispering. 'I'll see you in a minute.'

'OK. See you, then.' Anna stepped over Natalie on her way to the door and suddenly felt sorry that she had shouted at her. 'You coming, Nat?' she asked.

The laughter doubled up on itself. Anna turned away so they wouldn't see her blush. Why did she keep saying that?

'OK. Wait for me,' Natalie said, standing up and brushing the crisp bits off her jeans.

'And me.' Diane stood up and joined Anna at the door. 'Let's go, then.'

Natalie scurried after Di and Anna. Even harsh lights cast shadows and she did not want to be left in the long corridor by herself.

'Anna? It feels really weird . . .' she started to say and then checked herself. 'I mean, can I stay with you for a while if I promise not to talk about it?'

It was nice of Anna and Di to let her stay with them even for a bit, Natalie thought, as she reluctantly returned to her room. They were right. It probably wasn't a good idea to discuss it too much. On her own now, she found the story telling and re-telling itself in her head and, as it spun away from the facts, she became more and more afraid. You could hear the wind and the nasty big pine trees swishing about outside. It was all right for them. They wouldn't have to be alone. But Natalie didn't share a room with anyone – for the simple reason no one had been willing to share with her. Yes, she would have liked to have stayed a while longer, but she knew Diane and Michaela didn't like her. And Anna? She knew that the apparent friendliness could change in a second and her fear of mockery and cold rejection was greater than her fear of being alone.

She told herself she was just being silly. Things would seem different in the morning after a good night's sleep. She fancied a piece of chocolate and was wondering if she had any left, when a scuffling noise transfixed her. The part of her brain that could still think told her it came from the wardrobe. She watched, quite frozen, as a hand from the inside turned the knob on the door.

'Christ, what the bloody hell was that?'

Anna was the first to speak. The rending scream held them in freeze frame. They listened to the siren wail of pleading and anguish unable to move.

'Who is it?' Anna bent forward slightly, trying to identify the distorted voice behind the sound. 'Sounds like Natalie. Quick . . .'

She turned towards Diane and Michaela letting her words hang in the air.

'You go if you like, Anna,' Diane shuddered and

moved closer to Michaela. 'But I'm not going out there. Not after what we just heard.'

'Me neither,' Michaela breathed, her face was clay coloured against her bright bleached hair.

'We ought to do something,' Anna insisted. 'Anyway – it can't be the same thing, can it? Can't be outside and at the same time down the corridor.'

'You go and see then, if you're that interested. But we're not going,' Diane was shouting now, her voice edging up into hysteria. 'We're staying right here!'

'OK. I will,' Anna said and left the room.

She had to fight her way through the crowd thronged round Natalie's door.

'Show's over,' Ms Steadman was saying. She leant on the door jamb, barring the room. 'Just another stupid prank, wasn't it, Gary? Hiding in the wardrobe, jumping out and scaring the living daylights out of Natalie – just Gary's idea of a joke.' He stood with his head down, smirking. 'It's not funny, Gary. I'm not laughing.'

Anna felt her own mouth twitch as she imagined him, coiled in the dark waiting, then leaping out, festooned in dingy vests and bras, and the look of fear on Natalie's face. She bit back her own hysteria.

'Just a minute.' As Gary made his way past her, Ms Steadman held on to his arm.

'What?' Gary sneered down at her.

'Apologize to her,' Ms Steadman said.

'Soz, Nat,' he threw over his shoulder.

'I'm sorry, Gary,' the teacher's voice was quiet with unexpressed anger, 'but that's not good enough.'

Gary's thin gangly body tautened as Ms Steadman's grip on his arm tightened. For one heart stopping moment, Anna thought he might throw her off.

'You heard the lady, Gaz,' Andy's voice cut through the expectant silence. 'Do what she says and do it properly this time.'

'It's got nothing to do with you!' Gary's voice broke high in rage and humiliation.

'Do it!' Andy's eyes were like blue steel.

'I don't need your intervention, Andrew,' Ms Steadman said. But Gary had already jerked past her to apologize. Ms Steadman let him go and glared at the others.

'If I could, I'd pack the lot of you back – right now. Drive all through the night. I'd do it with pleasure. I've had just about enough!' She raked her hands through her hair. 'Now all of you, get back to bed! Your own bed,' she said, looking at Andy, 'in your own room. *Now!* Not you three – I want you to help me with Natalie.'

Anna, Di and Michaela watched the rest of them leave.

'Just a minute, Miss.' Diane touched her arm. She looked much younger without her make-up, bony knees stuck out from under her short nightdress. She was twisting some of the material round and round in her hand. 'There's something you ought to know. Before this Anna and Mick, all of us, heard this noise.'

Michaela looked as scared as Diane. Anna didn't appear to be frightened but she was just as serious. Liz knew that beneath the outward posing, Anna was sensible and highly intelligent. Her judgement could be trusted.

'What sort of noise?' Liz Steadman asked quietly.

'A sort of thumping.' Diane went on. 'A sort of scratching and thumping.' The other two nodded confirmation. 'It was coming from right under our window. We're down in the end bit, under the trees. It was quiet but,' her brow furrowed as she groped for the right word, 'persistent.' The sudden flare of fear was reflected in the

76

eyes of the others. 'It sounded like someone was trying to get in.'

'You all heard this?' the teacher said, looking from one to the other.

They nodded. They had handed her the problem. Now they stood waiting for her to know what to do.

'Right,' she said. 'Diane and Michaela, take Natalie back to your room. She can stay with you for tonight. Anna, you come with me. The police are keeping an eye on the place but we better make sure that everything is secure. Mr Peters can have a look around outside when he gets back. There's bound to be a simple explanation. This whole thing is getting way out of proportion. There is nothing to worry about, I'm sure.'

The girls nodded. They were not so certain. They would do what she told them but they sensed that, whatever her words said, she was not sure at all.

Chapter 13

'Oh – and what's going on here?'

Anna stood at the door of the community room and snapped the light on. She grinned down at Chris and Andy on the sagging settee.

'What's it frigging look like?' Andy sounded startled and angry. 'Turn the bloody light off, Anna, and stop pratting about!'

'What are you doing here, Anna?' Chris said, trying for 'cool' but getting 'guilty' instead.

'Not looking for you, if that's what you think. I'm helping Ms Steadman check all the doors and windows,' Anna said. As she went round the room, she watched them reflected in the blackness of the windows. 'Have you seen anyone? Don't suppose you have. Has anyone seen you? Maybe that's more to the point.'

'No, we haven't. Now bugger off and leave us alone! Oh – er – hi, Ms Steadman.' Andy scrambled off the settee and brushed a hand through his short fair hair. 'Didn't see you there. Chris thought she'd lost something down here and . . .'

'You were just helping her find it. How chivalrous of you, Andrew,' Ms Steadman said as she came into the room. 'I'm so glad I found you. You're just the person I'm looking for. There's a little job I'd like you to do. Go and find Mr Peters, he's just come back from the village, say that some of the girls heard noises outside and that I'd like the two of you to go and check it out. Make sure there's no one lurking about. Just you, Andy,' she added as he glanced at Chris, 'Christina stays with me.'

'Anything you say, Miss,' he said with his most charming smile. 'You're the boss.'

'Good. As long as that's understood.' Her smile was as false and as barbed as his own. 'Oh, Andy? Tuck your shirt in before you go.'

He turned his back on them and unzipped his jeans, taking his time to tuck in the stray shirt tail. The black windows were a perfect mirror.

Arrogant little bastard, Liz thought. Teachers were not supposed to have preferences, likes and dislikes, but of course they did. She remembered him coming into the school, his family having moved up from somewhere in the south-east. Attractive looking kid, bigger than most in his year. Not anything special academically but a talented sportsman, his physical maturity and relative sophistication had drawn admiration from boys and girls alike. He had been quick to use the power this had given him to bully and dominate. She could see him in the classroom, tipped back on his chair, the long muscles of his thighs controlling the chair's gentle rock. He had been pretty rather than handsome then, but his eyes had watched the class with an adult cruelty. His own friends were older. He had seen these as little kids, potential slaves and servants. They had courted him at first, seeking to please and impress. Then none of them had dared to meet his eyes or look directly at him. She had known what he was from that moment on, but she had never been able to catch him at it. One or two little lads, pushed to the edge, had sobbed out stories of constant intimidation and casual humiliation, but they had always denied them later, terrified in case he found out they'd grassed on him. He was nearly a man now and, according to the

79

headmaster, a credit to the school. So, what's new? But you'd think a girl like Chris O'Neill would be able to see through him.

'OK, Andy. You can put her down now,' she said.

Chris blushed.

'I'll say goodnight, then.' Andy grinned at them and sauntered out.

'It's all right, girls,' Ms Steadman said when she judged that he had finally gone. 'I'll do the rest.'

The two girls said goodnight and left Liz Steadman sitting on the lumpy settee with her eyes closed.

'Sorry about that,' Anna's voice came back through the open door.

'No you're not,' Chris laughed, 'you're not sorry at all. Doesn't matter. I was glad you came in, actually.'

'Oh, yeah? Getting a bit heavy was it?'

'Nothing I can't handle,' Chris replied.

'Yeah?' Anna laughed, 'Looked like it. I'd rather take my chances outside with a maniac than in there with him. Look, Chris. I really am sorry about, you know, earlier.'

'That makes two of us.'

'It just hit a nerve.'

'Want to tell me about it?'

'No.' Anna's response was automatic. The look on Chris's face gave the tension that had been winding her up all evening another twist. She couldn't take another row. Maybe it would help to talk about Paul, and she badly needed to feel close to Chris. 'Yeah. Yeah, I do.' Her breath came out in a rush. 'It was last year, when I went to Greece. My mother didn't want me to go. Sometimes mothers know best – you know?'

Liz stretched out on the settee as the conversation tailed off out of ear shot. She liked those two. She remembered the first time she had seen them. It had been her first class in a new school. Rows of anxious faces turned up to her as she came into the room. Second or third row back, they had been together even then. She had noticed Anna first, dark eyes, huge in her elfin face, peering up at her through a mass of glossy black curls. Liz had said something about being nervous too, about it being her first day as well, and Anna had smiled. She still had that same dazzling smile, but people saw it less often now. Since then Anna had gained a reputation for being difficult, arrogant and moody. Liz suspected that it was because the girl's powerfully intelligent and original mind was going its own way, refusing to accept or conform to the tired old stereotypes peddled by some of her colleagues. She wore her hair long now, a mane of black curls, and she was almost as tall as Liz herself with the slender but strong build of a natural athlete.

Chris had looked like a first-year angel. A natural for the angel Gabriel in that year's Rock Nativity; thick waving blonde hair tumbling on to her shoulders and wide-open, wide-apart eyes that changed from blue to green, depending on the light. Her hair was cut fashionably short now and her eyes were far less candid; her little girl prettiness was turning into something else altogether. Her ready smile was as charming and beguiling as ever. The Staff Room opinion, which had become so critical of Anna, was still effusive about Chris: 'Such a lovely girl', 'A pleasure to teach', 'Wish they were all like Chris O'Neill'. There would have been a few sharp intakes of breath if they had seen her a few minutes ago, wrapped like cling film round Andrew Henderson. Her dad was on the board of governors! She was not as tall as Anna, and there was a languid, almost fey quality about her. Definitely not the outdoor type.

Watching them grow up into attractive young women,

bright, intelligent, full of promise, that's what makes this shitty job worthwhile, she thought. Well, almost.

They were always together, had always been friends. There had been the odd falling out, a day or two sitting apart and not speaking, but it never lasted. They always drifted back to each other. Liz admired and slightly envied the strength of their friendship. She could see it stretching on into their adult lives, until Andrew Henderson was just a name from the past that they had to struggle to remember.

Somewhere above her, someone coughed.

'Jesus!' she cried, 'you made me jump!'

'Sorry.' Andrew cleared his throat again. 'Mr Peters says to tell you everything's secure. We made a thorough check outside and you know that noise? It was just a bunch of sheep.' He laughed. 'Sheep outside and sheep upstairs, eh, Miss?'

'I guess you're right,' she said, managing to smile back. ''Night then, Andrew. And thanks.'

'That's OK,' he shrugged his shoulders. He didn't like Steadman but he liked to take on responsibilities that the others were not given. That way they had to treat you equal, treat you like a man. He'd never act stupid like that tosser Gary. It was OK to do stuff but you had to keep it hidden, make sure they didn't find out. 'If there's nothing else, I'll say goodnight.'

'Can't think of anything. Goodnight, Andy.'

When he had gone she stretched out again and closed her eyes, mentally checking off that everything possible had been done to guarantee their safety. Nothing outside, every door and window secured against possible entry, to get in here now, he'd have to be able to de-materialize. The police were keeping a watch on the house. What's-his-name, Wainwright, had assured them of that. Low profile surveillance was the term he'd used. Don't expect too much contact. We don't want to alert him to our presence, but if you see anything suspicious, use this contact number, don't hesitate.

Then, this morning, another one turns up, telling them to get out, to leave immediately. What did he think they were on, a Sunday school outing? Had he any idea of what went into a trip like this? What was at stake? That was not an option, she had told him. It was out of the question. He'd told her, in that case, to make sure they locked all doors and windows. How many times did they have to be told that? And what was he doing there, anyway, if they weren't supposed to be contacted? It didn't exactly inspire confidence. Typical case of the right hand not knowing what the left is doing, just like school.

Who was this man, this anonymous 'Him', of whom they were all so terrified? He hadn't seemed real until Natalie had shown her that newspaper article. Even then there was nothing about him in it. It had all been about the girl. Still it had brought it home to her, the danger they were in. She sat up suddenly, and saw her face at the window, staring back, white and scored with worry lines. She jumped and the image started. This is getting silly now, she thought. I'm getting as bad as Diane and her sheep.

It was impossible. Like she had said, there was too much at stake, but she was having a hard time fighting down an impulse to follow the advice of the second policeman: pack up the buses, drive through the night, get them out of there. She passed her hand over her eyes. Anything would be better than this feeling that they were some kind of bait, sitting tethered and helpless, right in the middle of a nameless predator's hunting ground.

Chapter 14

It was like coming home, even though he was banished to the outer darkness of the hills. He had cut through the rough stems of the heather with his knife. He had to be careful. The thin stiletto blade was not suited to this kind of work. When he had enough he covered it with soft fronds of bracken like Gwyn had shown him and made it all into a bed, on the ledge he had selected, high above the house.

Coming to the house was the first thing he remembered. In his mind he saw the big front door, heard the bell ringing deep inside. It had been raining. Water dripped on to his head as they waited for someone to come. He looked up and saw his hand disappearing into a bigger one that extended from a grey sodden raincoat sleeve. Before that moment there was nothing. The memories of his real home, of his own parents and brothers and sisters, were not lost somewhere or buried but eaten up. They did not exist.

This was the only place where he could feel real. Here he was his true self. The first time he had come back as a man he had expected it to be the same, even though he had been there when the funding ran out and all the kids, including himself, had been shipped off to foster homes. At the first one he'd gone to, the woman had been nice enough, but she had enough kids of her own, and couldn't cope. The gas fire and the nappies smelling made him want to puke all the time. Then they'd sent him to a right cow – only did it for the money, only gave him one blanket all that cold winter, called the social worker because, she said, he 'stole' a slice of bread. But it didn't matter because he always kept this place safe inside his head. And later when things got bad, and awful things started to happen, he had come back again. It had been boarded-up but that did not matter. Better really, to have the place to himself except for the skittering in the skirting boards and the bats that hung in the roof. He had sat in the dark, listening to the rain drum and the whisper of the fire in the grate, feeling safe and real for the first time in years.

This time he had come back to find that the house was not empty. He'd tried to get rid of them. When he got back from the seaside and they were not there, he'd hoped it could be like it was before. But then a minibus had turned into the drive, spraying gravel, kicking up dust and the kids came tumbling out, shouting and screaming. A couple of them had started kicking a can around, trampling the few spring flowers into the crisp packets and sweet wrappers that littered up the place. Everything was spoilt, and it was all their fault. They were an infestation, crawling all over the place like parasites.

They had failed to take his advice, and he was mad about that, but they were scared all right. He had watched lights going on and off in random patterns, chasing through the house below him, with growing excitement. It was like an automatic alarm system triggered by the fear he had planted there. Even now thin pencils of torch light flicked round the garden. In the stillness he had heard them calling, first a man and then, in reply, a boy's higher voice. They could search all they liked, they'd never find how he left and entered. Any time, day or night, he could come and go as he pleased and it wouldn't be long now, he'd have them out of there.

It was really just the beginning. He must control the urgency that was surging through him, try not to act impulsively. He must let it work slowly, let it work in its own way, fermenting like yeast within them. On the thin wind blowing up from the valley he thought he could already smell the sweet sharp scent of fear.

Chapter 15

'If he does that to me,' Diane muttered, 'I'm going to drop the bastard!'

Day two: Rough Terrain/Mountain Activities. They had been walking all morning. It was still unseasonably hot for the time of year and the girls sweated in a line along a narrow gorge, trying not to look down at the white water churning and gurgling below them. The path they had been following had given out altogether, blocked by a large boulder. They would have to wait for Peters to help them round.

Anna squinted up ahead, 'Who?'

'Peters – look – he's even touching Natalie up!' Diane spat. Chomped bubble gum lay between her boots like a fluorescent worm.

Natalie scrabbled round, with Peters' big hand squarely on her bum.

Anna laughed. 'He's only helping her. What else is he going to use? It sticks out far enough. Biggest thrill she'll get all week.'

'Well, he won't cop a thrill off me.' Diane broke out some fresh gum. 'He doesn't do that to the boys.'

'No, he just pushed them in,' Michaela said, peering down at Colin struggling out of the water. He was Peters's latest victim, pitched off into the deep pool that lay directly below the obstructing boulder. 'We had a dog looked like that, a bull terrier, ran to fat. Dad had it put down. I hate wearing these things.' She fiddled with the strap of her safety helmet. 'They really itch me.'

'Better than something falling on your head,' Anna said, adjusting her own strap.

'Wouldn't make much difference to her if it did,' Diane's laugh brayed away on the wind.

'I'm sick of you!' Michaela screamed viciously and lunged at Diane.

Diane slipped, scree bounced down and chocked into the stream. She grabbed on to Chris to save herself and more of the slaty path fell away from under their feet.

'Pack it in, will you!' Anna shouted, pulling them roughly back into line. 'We don't need to try them out! Are you all right, Chris?'

Chris had gone very white, but she nodded. Anna squeezed her arm and tried to smile reassurance, she knew that Chris had not been looking forward to this.

'It's your turn, Di,' she said, indicating Peters' beckoning hand. 'Go on, give it to him.'

'Don't worry,' Diane said, straightening her shoulders. 'You just watch him go!'

Peters didn't even pretend to help Diane. He had her off the rock and into the water in seconds and stood, arms folded, laughing down at her. Applause and whistles echoed back from further up the gorge and added to the noise Diane was making, swearing and splashing around. She was having problems getting out but no one was exactly rushing to help.

'It's your turn, Anna,' Peters was shouting for her, laughing, smoothing down his moustache.

'Right, Mr Peters, you bastard,' she muttered through smiling teeth.

Anna swung down the path towards him, perfectly balanced. Chris hung on to Michaela and watched her go.

Anna received more help than most from Peters. He caged her body with his own, pressing hard against her. When she was sufficiently sure of her purchase on the rock's slippery surface, she flexed her knees and thrust out and back with her hips. The movement was very quick, then she was plastered on the rock again, edging her way back to come and help them round.

A very loud splash swallowed his roaring shout. Delighted cheers and laughter filled the gorge. Anna stepped away from the rock and acknowledged the applause with a mock bow.

'It was great what you did back there,' Diane said as she opened one of her hard crusty batches to examine its contents. Her clothes were drying on her in the hot midday sun. 'You're the only one who could have done it except Steadman and she wouldn't.'

'Why not?' Anna leaned back into the rough grass, closing her eyes. 'She doesn't like him much either.'

'Nah – she wouldn't,' Diane shook her head. 'She's a teacher.'

Diane stared down at Anna, studying her. Even here with all that climbing gear on she looked like a model on location. She never seemed to bother much, but she always looked good. Diane was not happy with herself unless she was in her tightest jeans or a really short skirt and high heels, her face masked with make-up. Without all that, she privately considered she looked rather like a hamster, she certainly felt like one.

'You like all this here, don't you?' she said suddenly. 'The climbing and that?'

Anna sat up and hugged her knees. She watched the small figures, like action-men dolls, strung along the bright threads of rope that criss-crossed the great grey wall of rock opposite them. She was edging up there with them; enjoying the risk, feeling the tense sense of control and physical excitement that gave her the high.

'Yes,' she said simply, 'yes, I do.'

From behind them came snorting and shrieking. Andy and Chris were rolling over and over on the hillside above them. Andy was pouncing on her, biting at her neck, making deep roaring animal noises. While Chris, faking escape, lay helpless with laughter.

'I think he really likes her,' Diane said miserably.

'Looks like he's going to eat her.'

Anna turned from watching them to feeding the sheep that were standing around eyeing their packed lunches. Anna offered a bit of bright pink salami to one of them but it wrinkled up its nose and spat it out.

'I wonder if ponies like salami?' she said, nodding towards some ponies, grouped a short distance away, cropping at the short tough grass.

'I shouldn't think so,' Diane laughed, 'probably one of their relations. They prefer just bread.'

She got up quietly and slowly approached them, tearing her batch into little pieces. She held her hand out flat, calling, 'Ch, ch, ch, c'mon, c'mon.' The boldest of the ponies came shyly towards her and started to nuzzle at the bits of bread with its soft velvety mouth. Diane stroked the pony's nose and then threw the rest of the bread on the ground for the others.

'Used to have a pony myself once, when I was little,' she said when she came back.

'Funny,' Anna smiled, one thick black eyebrow quirked up, 'I'd never have taken you for the horse-riding type.'

'There you go,' Diane grinned, 'had all the kit too. About ten I was, pony mad. He was a real sweet pony, not very big, and ever so gentle.' Diane's dark eyes filled with remembering and then she started to laugh.

She laughed so hard that all the sheep scattered. She rolled around and beat her fists.

'What is it, Di?' Anna shook her, laughing herself now, not knowing what they were laughing about. 'What's so funny?'

'It's the pony's name!' Diane squeaked out, almost incoherent. 'I just remembered, his name was Andy. The pony's bloody name was Andy!' She beat it like a tattoo on the ground.

They were both swept into laughter that went on and on until it was almost unbearable. They had to hold on to themselves to stop from breaking apart. Finally they lay together breathless and shaking.

'What happened to him?' Anna gasped. 'What happened to the pony?'

'Oh,' Diane sniffed back the tears and wiped her eyes. 'We had to get rid of him, my dad said we couldn't afford him any more. Cried my eyes out when we sold him.' She coughed and laughed again, shakily. 'Then I discovered boys.'

When they were quiet, the mountain ponies came slowly back and stood quite near them. Anna went over and offered some of her batch in the way that Diane showed her.

'Oh!' Anna shivered as one of the ponies delicately took the food. 'Feels all soft and wet!'

'Bit like Andy,' Diane said.

Again, Anna felt the laughter bubbling up between them as they returned to their picnic, but this time it died away as the mood change moved like a cloud across Diane's face.

'He's a real sod, Anna. I mean it,' she said, glancing up

at the hillside above them, suddenly troubled and serious. 'You've got to warn her before it's too late.'

'I have,' Anna replied softly. 'She won't take any notice.'

'I've been with him, y'know. A couple of times. Well, more than a couple of times. And the next day – he won't even acknowledge you, won't even say "hello" or anything. Just stands around laughing, letting his mates call you a slag.' Anna stared at the climbers on the opposite side of the valley as Diane struggled with the tears in her voice. 'He really uses people. Not just him, they all do. They're all the bloody same. But he's the worst.'

'Why do you let them, Di?' Anna's quiet voice cut into the other girl's silence. 'Why do you let them do it to you?'

Diane laughed, hard and sharp. 'Once you've done it, it's difficult to say No. I mean, what reason could you give?'

'What do you mean, "what reason"?' Anna's voice was edging into anger. 'Why should you have to give a reason? Say you don't want to. Say you don't fancy it. Tell them to piss off! You shouldn't have to give a reason, for Christ's sake!'

'Saying No isn't worth the hassle. They'd call you a slag in any case.' She regarded Anna curiously, wondering, for a moment, exactly who she was talking about. Laughter gusted down to them on the wind. 'Anyway,' she sighed, 'I fancy him. So I think if I go with him, then maybe one day he'll go out with me – properly, like.'

But Anna seemed to have stopped listening. She sat staring straight ahead, chin on her knees, lost in her own thoughts.

Chapter 16

Andy and Chris were split up for that afternoon's activities. Andy went off with Steadman and the advanced climbers. Chris, who hated climbing and was afraid of heights, had to stay with Peters. She felt slightly better about it when she knew that Anna and Mark had volunteered to stay behind and help him with the novices.

Andy normally loved mountain work but this afternoon he couldn't wait for it to be over. He hung on the face not feeling there half the time, thinking about Chris, not knowing what the hell he was doing. He just wanted to get back to her so they could spend time together. Trust Steadman to take the rubbish bus, he thought on the slow return journey. This one couldn't cope with the terrain, it was going to take for ever. It was not until he saw the sign for the Visitors' Centre that he started to relax. He scanned the car park for the other group but as soon as he saw them he was out of his seat and leaping down the aisle. He wrenched back the door and, before the bus had properly come to a halt, he was off and running.

'What the hell do you think you're doing?'

At the sound of Andy's voice, friendly words of reassurance died in Mark's mouth. His arm dropped from Chris's shoulder as though he had been stung.

'Nothing, Hendy. Honest!' Mark's voice broke up into a squeak and his big honest face dulled crimson. He looked round for support but they all turned away from him and got on with what they were doing. Gary coiled and re-coiled the rope he was carrying and Colin helped him pack the climbing gear into the back of the bus. No one in their right mind would try to tackle Andy in that sort of mood. Dave sauntered off to find the others.

'You!' Andy turned his white-faced shaking fury on to Chris. 'Come here!'

He grabbed her arm and dragged her away from them across the car park.

'It's not what it looks like,' Mark shouted after them, his bruised and grazed hands held up in despair. 'It's not what you think!'

Andy ignored the people staring after them, peering curiously from their cars, sandwiches arrested half-way to their mouths. Violent outbursts were rare in beauty-spot car parks. This was an unexpected treat. They watched to see what would happen next.

When he considered that they were far enough away from the others, Andy pushed Chris up against a stone wall and held her captive there. His arms pinned her shoulders, his hands caged her head. He was mottling up red and his wide-spaced blue eyes had gone opaque. A thick vein wormed in his temple under a film of sweat.

Chris breathed a fine spray of his saliva as he shouted into her face. She had never been close up to anyone this angry, certainly not this angry with her, and she did not like it.

'The minute my back's turned you're off with someone else!' he was screaming. 'I don't believe this! Why are you doing this to me! You're just like all the rest. I thought you were different, but you're not – you're just as much of a . . .'

'Now, hold on just a minute, Andy!' she shouted back against his torrent of abuse. 'Listen to me! It's nothing like what you're thinking!'

But he was not listening. He smothered her words with more of his own. Chris could hardly recognize him. Through her thin shirt she could feel the sharp stones cutting into her skin, bruising her flesh. She wondered if it would mark her, if it would show. It was still hot but cold sweat was creeping across her forehead and upper lip.

She felt like she was on that rock again.

Earlier in the afternoon she had got herself stuck half-way up a rock face. It was supposed to be dead easy, a beginners' face, but there she was. Her fingers and toes had frozen themselves into the crevices and she had been fixed half-way, unable to move up or down or in any direction. Stuck in the middle of a sunny afternoon.

For a moment she was able to hear everything: Anna shouting down to her, Mark shouting something else from below, Mr Peters booming at her from some other place. But she could not recognize what they were saying, the words came and went on the wind and did not make sense. The only thing she heard with clear understanding was Diane whimpering right below her, fear whispering up to meet her own.

A stone scutters down the rock face and another sound fills her ears. She doesn't know if it's the wind or her own voice hitting one high-pitched note.

Then all sound recedes. She is in the silent place with the words which need no voice. The words that tell her what to do, what she really wants to do, what she knew she would want to do – the thing she always wants to do in high places.

The words become the beat and roar of her own blood. The rock in front of her and the snake of striped nylon rope appear very near and then far away. Incredibly near, then far away. All she has to do is let go and fall and fall and fall.

'Hold on. Hang on in there.' Mark's words came soft and warm as his breath on her neck. 'Soon get you out of this.'

'For God's sake, Chris. Don't let go. You'll take me with you!' Diane called from beneath her feet.

'Shut it, Di,' Mark growled. 'You'll make her worse.'

'I'm just as scared you know!'

'Yeah? Well, you'll have to wait. I can only cope with one at a time.'

'Bloody typical!' Diane whined on. 'She always gets all the attention. Done it on purpose, I reckon.'

'If you don't shut up,' Mark shouted down to her, 'I'm gonna come and push you off myself. Give it a rest, Di. If I can free her up you can all get moving. Now then, Chrissy, you listen to me . . .'

Slowly, with infinite and gentle patience, he talked to her. His rough voice coaxed her out of the freezing place. She had been able to move and see his face then, big and familiar, next to hers. He grinned his big white-toothed grin, his blue eyes were flecked with fear and laughter at the same time. He had free-climbed up to her, and talked her up the rest of the way. He had saved her. And now Andy was shouting terrible things about him.

As far back as she could remember, Chris had been afraid of heights. One of her earliest memories was of being whirled up into the air by a giant of an uncle and placed, like a small jockey, on his shoulders. She was very little, with no words to speak her fear or to demand to be returned to the safe flat ground. She had been too frightened to scream. She remembered the ungainly bumping, like being on an animal that is not designed to bear another – an elephant or a kangaroo. She was too near the trees and could see over walls that she had not even realized had tops to them. She was just as suddenly returned to the ground, legs like rubber, knickers warm and wet. Her mother was apologizing, 'She's usually so good – been out of nappies for ages.' Chris was looking down at strands of her uncle's curly hair, stuck like red wire in the grey crinkled lines of her hand. The fear is the same now as it was then, there is no way she can make it less. Why can't he understand that? Anna and Mark understood.

But Andy did not understand, and Chris could not even be bothered to find words to stem this torrent of abuse. She closed her eyes against him and saw Anna leaning out over the top of the ridge to get her. She felt Anna's strength pulling her up, felt her arms go round her, holding her. Her legs were trembling so much she could hardly walk as Anna led her away from the edge. Peters had swallowed his anger at the chaos she had caused, at the danger Mark and Anna had put themselves into. He had looked her over anxiously, chewing his moustache, and had given her brandy from a small silver flask he carried. Even he had understood. Andy did not understand. He had not understood earlier, before the hideous climb, when she had tried to explain to him how she felt. It was easy, he had said, easy as climbing a ladder. What did he know about how she felt on ladders?

'I nearly fell,' she finally said. 'Mark helped me. He was seeing if I was all right, that's all. Now excuse me.'

She pushed him aside. She could swallow back the saliva no longer, she had to get away from him. She made it to the end of the wall and then, hanging on the rough-edged stone, she was violently sick.

*

'Chris, Chris,' someone was shaking her, 'are you all right?'

She opened her eyes and looked around. She was sitting on the ground, not far from where they had been, but Andy was nowhere to be seen. It was Natalie's face that came looming over her.

'No, I don't think I am.' Chris struggled to sit up and everything swam. 'I think I passed out or something.'

'Here. Put your head between your knees. That's what my mum says to do. I'll go and get someone.'

Before she could stop her Natalie had raced away. Chris had to focus on individual pieces of gravel to stop everything whirling and spinning again.

'Here she is, Miss.'

Ms Steadman knelt in front of her and gently raised her head. She pushed Chris's hair back and looked into her eyes and then felt her pulse.

'How are you feeling? Have you been sick?'

She nodded.

'Could be too much sun. Or' – Ms Steadman frowned, surveying her with renewed concern – 'when you were climbing with Mr Peters' group, did you hit your head at all?'

'I don't remember.' Chris's voice was weak and small.

The teacher stood up decisively. 'Could be concussion. I'm going to take you back.' She reached down and helped Chris to her feet. 'I don't like the look of this.'

'I'll come with her,' Natalie said, moving in to support her on the other side.

'No, Natalie. You go and find Mr Peters, while I round up my group. Tell him I'm going back. Come on, Chris.'

*

Ms Steadman gave orders for the others to unload the bus and took Chris into the house. It was a relief to leave the glare of the afternoon. Chris imagined she caught the faintest scent of furniture polish as she stepped into the hall. When they were not there, she thought, perhaps trace memories of what the house had once been were allowed to surface.

'How do you feel now?' Ms Steadman asked briskly.

'Oh,' Chris shrugged. 'Not so bad. I don't feel faint now. I've just got a bit of a headache.'

'Right. You sit down there,' Ms Steadman said, indicating a chair in the middle of the hall. 'And I'll get you something for it.'

When she came back the chair was back in its usual place against the wall and Chris was sitting on the stairs, paler than she was before. Freckles showed like a spatter of tea leaves across her nose and her face was the colour of a crêpe bandage.

Ms Steadman sat down next to her and gave her the glass she carried.

'What's the matter?' she said. 'Do you feel faint again?'

'No.' Chris shook her head. 'It's not that. I found this on the chair, Ms Steadman.'

The loosely folded paper trembled as Chris handed it to her. Ms Steadman took it and flattened it out on the knee of her jeans.

I TOLD YOU – LOCK ALL DOORS AND
WINDOWS

Uneven capitals written with smudgy biro on white paper with thin blue lines. The top edge was jagged where it had been torn from a notebook. She turned it over in her hands. That was all it said. It had been placed on that chair which had been carefully and deliberately put in the middle of the hall.

'That chair, where you found it,' she said to Chris, 'do you remember it being in that position this morning?'

Chris shook her head.

Ms Steadman bit her lip. So if it hadn't been like that when they left, it meant it had to have been put there some time when they were out. She had checked and re-checked every door, every window. There was no way in. She could have sworn it. So how could it have got there? And, what was more to the point, who had put it there?

It could be a hoax, she told herself. But there was simply no way that any of the children could have put it there, and it wouldn't have been Mike Peters and it certainly wasn't her. Who did that leave?

'What do you think, Miss?' Chris was shaking her arm. 'How did it get there? Who could have done it?'

'What? Oh, I don't know.' She paused for a second and then said, 'Could be the police, I suppose. The one that was here yesterday morning. He even said that, make sure you lock all doors and windows.'

'Oh yeah,' Chris said, 'could be. I saw him later, at the fairground, but I couldn't place where I'd seen him. Maybe he's supposed to be keeping an eye on us.'

'Are you sure it was him?' Ms Steadman asked sharply.

'Yes, I think so. He had funny-coloured eyes, didn't you notice? Really unusual.'

'Have you seen him again?'

Chris shook her head.

'A bit of a weird thing to do, isn't it, Miss? I mean, that's not exactly what they're supposed to do, is it? Go round scaring people.'

'Maybe he meant us to take it as a warning to be more vigilant. But you're right, it is rather strange.' Ms Steadman folded the note and put it in her pocket. 'At the very least it's unorthodox.' She stood up and helped Chris to her feet. 'We are going to have the rest of them crashing in any minute, you take a couple of these and go and lie down. And Chris, I'd prefer it if you'd keep this to yourself, just until I've been able to get on to the police and check into it.'

Chapter 17

'Chris, open the door. It's me, Anna.'

'Christ, you look terrible,' Anna said when she let her in. 'How do you feel?'

Before Chris could tell her there was another knock at the door.

'Chris? Are you there? I've got to see you.'

'It's Andy,' Chris shook her head frantically. 'I don't want to see him, Anna. Don't let him in.'

'Don't worry.' Anna went back to the door. 'I'll deal with him.'

'I just want to see her, Anna. Just for a minute.'

Andy confronted her, square and adamant. He was not used to opposition, he was used to getting his own way.

'What for? To push her around some more? Maybe beat up on her a little bit?' Anna's sarcasm corroded the air between them. 'I heard about that and I wasn't impressed. Go away. She doesn't want to see you. She just wants to be left alone.'

'Oh, yeah?' he said, his mouth twisting into a sneering smile.

'Yeah,' she smiled back, arms folded, regarding him with studied insolence, 'by everyone. Including you.' Her smile widened. 'Especially including you.'

They stared at each other. Andy's wide apart eyes were so close, she could see a webbing of bright red veins around the blue of the iris. A thin scar made one of his eyebrows crook up. His nose and cheeks were sprayed with freckles; maybe it was the sun of the day, or just that she had never been this close to him before. His skin was flawless, smooth as a girl's. He had nice teeth, white and even. She could see why some girls might think he was cute.

'She doesn't want to see you, Andy,' she said again, repeating the words with drawling contempt. 'So go away. Now if you'll excuse me, I've got better things to do.'

She turned to go back into the room, dismissing him.

'Well, we've only got your word for it, haven't we?' He glared round. Doors were folded shut, all down the corridor, like playing cards. 'She's seeing me!'

He wrenched Anna's hand off the door handle and was in the room.

Chris was not asleep, she lay with her eyes closed, ignoring them.

'I'm really sorry, Chrissy,' Anna said. 'I tried, honest.'

Chris nodded. She knew. There was silence in the room. Anna sighed, making up her mind.

'OK,' she said finally. 'I'll leave you then.'

The door closed and Anna's light footsteps walked away.

'How are you then? OK now?' The light metal frame creaked as he sat down on the edge of the bed. 'I had to see you, Chrissy. I heard what happened. And look, I'm sorry, I'm really sorry.'

He leaned over and kissed her, she turned her face away. Anna's travel alarm quietly ticked off the silence that thickened between them.

'Hi – I'm Andy. Remember?'

He reached towards her and started tickling her. It was like nothing had happened. She couldn't believe it. Her eyes snapped open.

103

'Pack that in, Andy! Cut it out! Just go away and leave me alone!'

He backed off, holding his hands up, palms out. 'OK, OK, I'm sorry, I'm sorry!'

She threw herself back into the pillow and burrowed away from him, face to the wall.

'What's wrong with you? I've said I'm sorry, and I am.' He pushed himself off the bed and paced the room. 'Look, it's just when I saw you with Mark, with his arm round your shoulder . . .' His voice shook and the breath rushed out of him. He was still struggling with something he found hard to control. 'It just freaked me out, that's all. I didn't understand, and now I do. I was out of order back there, I know that now. Well out of order. And I'm sorry. It won't happen again, I promise.' The pacing brought him back to the bed. 'Here, I've brought you something. You said you liked it.'

Chris sat up to see what he'd thrown at her. Milky Bars, Dairy Crunch, white chocolate bars of every kind, slipped and slithered away from her and settled in patterns all over the bed.

'Forgive me, please?' He sat down again, his blue eyes pleading. 'Please?'

Reluctantly her eyes met his. Despite the anger she felt about how he had treated her earlier, his solid presence felt warm and comforting. She could feel the ghost of a smile starting. His grin lit up the space between them as he leaned closer, trying to see into her face.

'That's better. Do you forgive me? No? Yes?' He tipped her chin, kissing her lightly and this time she didn't resist.

'I'll think about it,' she said when they eventually broke away from each other. 'Now, please go away. I feel exhausted, I need to get some sleep.'

'OK,' Andy shrugged and grinned, his confidence completely restored. 'So when will I see you? We're going down to the pub later with Peters. Want to come? Hey! What's this?'

'No, I really don't think so. Give me that!' Chris's tone changed from from indifference to panic as she saw what he held in his hand. 'It's my diary. Give it to me!' She made a swipe for it but he jerked it out of her reach. The duvet fell away as she made another desperate bid. Andy stopped looking at the book and gave a long whistle. Chris's blush was not limited to her face. She snatched the duvet back to cover her nakedness pulling it right up to her chin. 'Give it back, I'm not joking, Andy. Give it to me now!'

'It's locked.' Andy turned the diary over. He was in no hurry to return it and there was nothing she could do about it. 'Anything about me in it?'

'Yes – no – maybe, please, Andy.' She held out her hand.

'Can I read it?'

'No. No one is allowed to read it.'

'Not even Anna?'

Chris gasped. 'Especially not Anna. Now can I have it back – please!'

'OK.' He held the book just out of her reach and, as she went to take it, he pulled it away. 'Just wanted to see if you'd do it again. Tell you what,' he grinned, tapping the book on his chin, 'you can have it back if you promise to come with me tonight.'

'All right! Now give!'

'Great!' He threw the book back to her. 'That's great, Chris. I was hoping you would say yes. I mean, we haven't got much time left.'

'What do you mean?' Chris's voice was ice cold.

Andy shifted nervously, he sensed that he had not said the right thing. 'Well, I mean, in a couple of days, we'll be back . . .'

'A couple of days and we'll be back to what? Back to normal? Or you'll be back with Elaine. Is that what you mean?' Chris turned on him with real fury. 'You are really something else, you know that? Back in that car park, just this afternoon, you were shouting and shouting at me: "My girl does this", "My girl does not do that". And now it turns out that I'm just going to be "Your girl" for a couple of days. I should have really listened carefully to that tape you sent me, shouldn't I? I should have listened to it and thrown it in the bin with the rest of the garbage. All that stuff, how'd it go? Oh, yeah, "Believe me it wouldn't just be a short-term thing". Ha, ha!' Her laughter rang between them, hard and hollow.

'No! Chris, I didn't mean that! I . . .' Words were running out on him. They stared at each other across the room. He came back and sat on the side of the bed. 'It's not like that, honest! Look, Chris, I think, I really do think I . . .' He searched around helplessly, trembling on the brink of what he wanted to say. 'When I get back,' his voice was suddenly cold, 'I will tell Elaine. I'm finishing with her.'

'Don't finish with her for me.' Chris's words dropped like stones.

'What?'

'I said: Don't do it. Not for me.'

'Why not?'

Chris shrugged. 'Because it wouldn't be worth it.'

She sighed and shook her head. She should have said, she had intended to say: 'Because I don't want to go out with you', but when the time came the words didn't come out like that. Was she trying not to hurt him or was she just being a coward? Whichever. She knew that she would regret this. It was a mistake to lie that way.

'But it would be. It would be worth it to me.' He said it with such sincerity that she had to look away. 'What's wrong, Chrissy? I want you to tell me.'

He took her hand and held it tightly. She found it difficult to meet his gaze. His sudden intensity was unnerving her, making her swallow back the words she had been determined to say.

'Oh, look, I'm just knackered, that's all, I will come tonight – but you've got to promise me something.'

'What? Promise what? Anything.' He spread his hands wide. 'You can have anything!'

'That's just it!' She frowned at him. 'You don't understand, do you? It's too much. I don't want you to give me anything, and I don't want you to buy me anything. I mean, all this,' she pointed to the jumble of chocolate bars on the bed, 'it's nice and everything, but I'm not used to it. I tell you that I like Kendal Mint Cake, say, and the next thing I know, I've got enough to supply an Everest expedition. I don't think you mean it that way, but it feels like you're trying to buy me and I'm not for sale. I'll come with you tonight but leave me some room, all right? Now I really could use some sleep.'

'OK,' he grinned down at her and kissed her gently. 'Whatever you say. I'll be seeing you later. Have a good sleep.'

He winked at her and left the room. She wondered how much of what she had said he had actually heard. All through the conversation part of her had been listening to his taped voice looping on, not just a short-term thing . . . not just a short-term thing. He'd been using her. But, then, hadn't she allowed him to? And if she was honest, enjoyed it too. Or maybe she was using him? Who used

107

who when you got involved like this? She didn't know. Everything was moving too far, too fast for her to be certain of anything.

What about Elaine? What if he did finish with her? She saw a small dark-haired girl with a pleasant, pretty face. Chris did not know her very well but she seemed nice enough. Elaine was mad about Andy, they were an item. What would she think when she found out about this? Somebody is sure to tell her, Chris thought, I've probably caused real trouble already. I don't want to make it worse. I don't want to make someone else suffer. I'm not like that. 'Don't do it. Not for me. It's just not worth it,' she silently pleaded. 'But it is. Don't you see? It is for me.' Andy's voice whispered back. What did Andy feel about her that made him want to finish with Elaine, after so long? She did not feel ready to be the focus of that sort of emotion. It scared her to be wanted like that.

She must have fallen asleep. When she woke up the light had slid from the room but it had not taken the day's heat with it. The duvet lay crumpled on the floor. Chris touched her body, it was slick and wet. Sweat pooled between her breasts and her hair was stuck in damp ringlets to her forehead and neck. It was not the humid heat in the room that had made her sweat like this. Her breathing still came shallow as she lay remembering her dream. Sometimes when you sleep in the day, in the heat, when you sleep because you don't want to be awake, you have dreams like this, dreams that are more vivid than your waking existence. They live on in your mind, in every detail. They tell you things you didn't want to know.

She had been back in that car park with Andy. That part had been just the same, except the colours were all brighter and she could see every detail, see things she hadn't been able to see or hadn't consciously noticed before. She could see herself and be herself at the same time; see her head snap back and her shirt pull out of her jeans as he grabbed her, see her trainers scuffing the dirt as he dragged her along. She saw herself slamming up against the wall and felt the pain at the same time. But why it was happening was different. He was saving her, dragging her away from something. She felt the shiny spiky texture of his hair between her fingers, against her palms as she pulled his head down to hers. She touched her lips now, half surprised that they were not bruised and swollen, that no blood came away on her hand. She could see herself and she could see people watching with colourless eyes from cars defaced by blue graffiti scrawl: *all* doors, *all* windows. Their faces swam towards her like fish in an aquarium. She wanted it to happen. She had wanted Andy, wanted him to hold her, had not wanted him to stop.

Chris had never felt like that, not in real life. She had not believed herself to be capable of it. She reached for her diary and started to write. When she thought she had finished, she read through the last part again.

'In the dream it felt like when he held me I was safe, but from what? At the beginning I found all the attention he was giving me very flattering, but now it's smothering. The feeling of being looked after is certainly a novelty, but it could get addictive. And what about the other side of him: the possessiveness, jealousy, violence even? Is that the price you have to pay? Could you get to need it, find it exciting, even? Am I the kind to get off on that?'

*

There were too many questions and she didn't know the answers. She felt as if she was disintegrating, she didn't know herself any more. The whole thing scared her. She picked up her pen again.

'I should get out of it, right now, while I still can. I don't think I like feeling like this.'

Chapter 18

'It was a good idea to bring them down here,' Liz Steadman said as she finished her drink.

'Bloody stroke of genius.' Mike Peters licked the foam off his moustache. 'Want another? Same again?'

'Yes, thanks, Mike.'

Liz sat back in her chair and lit a cigarette. The small pub was packed now, with climbers and tourists crowding out the few locals, but she wondered how it made a living out of season in such an isolated place. The landlord had said it would be all right to bring them in as long as the younger ones stuck to soft drinks and the older ones stuck to halves and they didn't make too much noise. Most of the noise was coming from a group of climbers, occupying the large central table. There was a darts match going on in the corner with Anna and Mark captaining a team playing some kids from the Youth Hostel. Chris and Andy were on their own by the window, apart from the rest of the group. They bent towards each other, creating their own exclusion zone. That's still on then, she thought.

'You shouldn't smoke,' he said as he came back to their table. 'It's bad for you and a bad example to that lot.'

'I know.' Liz stubbed out her cigarette.

'Here you go then.' Mike put a pint of lager in front of her.

'Thanks,' she said, reaching in her bag. 'How much do I owe you?'

'Nothing. On me.' Mike took a long pull on his pint.

'Do a good pint here.' His blue eyes cast round constantly, searching for the first hint of trouble. 'Drawn from the wood. You ought to try it instead of that piss you're drinking.'

'No thanks.' Liz grimaced. 'I don't like bitter. Too claggy.'

'You don't know what you're missing. All quiet so far, eh? You can get the next ones in.'

They sat in silence that was not exactly companionable. They had nothing in common, apart from Outdoor Pursuits, and although Liz enjoyed teaching the subject, as a topic of conversation, it had its limitations. Besides that there was something she had to talk to him about and she couldn't put it off any longer. He wasn't going to like it, but that couldn't be helped.

'Ms Steadman.' Liz looked up into Chris O'Neill's best teacher-pleasing smile.

'Yes, Chris,' she smiled back. 'What can I do for you?'

'I was, uh, wondering if you would lend me some money to buy a drink?'

'Yes, of course.' Liz reached for her purse and handed her a five pound note. 'Haven't got any less, I'm afraid.'

'Thanks, I'll pay you back. It's my round you see,' her eyes indicated Andrew Henderson who was grinning back, 'and I forgot my money.'

'That's OK. Don't worry about it.' She didn't know what was going on but there was something about the way Andy was watching them that was making her feel uncomfortable too.

'How are you feeling now, Chris?' Mike Peters asked her. 'None the worse for it?'

'What?' Chris re-focused on Mr Peters. 'Oh, yes, thanks, I feel fine now. I'll bring you the change, Miss.'

'Pretty girl that,' he said as they watched her move away towards the bar.

'Yes, she is very pretty,' Liz agreed. Obviously the climbers thought so too, judging by the attention she was getting as she tried to squeeze by their table and the comments they were shouting after her. Over the other side of the room, Andy's eyes followed every move she made with disturbing intensity. 'What actually happened this afternoon, then?'

After a while Liz was only half listening. Mike Peters could make anything sound really boring.

'Here you are, Miss.' Chris rested her tray on their table and dug in her pockets for the change.

Liz looked at the handful of coins. 'It's not mine,' she said.

Chris frowned. Sometimes teachers were really weird. 'Yes it is. You just lent me a five pound note. That's the change.'

'Yes, I know. But then Andy came over and gave me this.' She waved a five pound note. 'So it's not mine, it's his. You'll have to give him the change, not me.'

'I see.' Chris struggled to keep her voice polite but anger surged into her eyes and a faint blush spread up her face. 'Thank you, Ms Steadman.'

Beer slopped as Chris steered through the crowd and heads turned as she banged the tray down on the table in front of Andy. Loose money scattered over him and rolled off across the floor. Chris kept her voice low but you could hear the fury way across the room. When she had had her say, she stalked away.

Andy took a drink from his pint, affecting indifference. But his hands were shaking and beer spilt down his shirt. He picked up a cigarette packet and crushed it in his

113

hand. His eyes never left her as she strode over to the dart board and snatched the darts from Anna. Darts thudded into the board, a shout of triumph went up around her. Lucky shots, she hadn't even been looking.

'What was that all about?' Mike Peters turned to Liz with a puzzled frown.

'Search me,' Liz shrugged. She clicked her empty glass against his. 'Want another? Same again?' Peters looked at his watch. 'There's plenty of time. Besides, I owe you one – and there's something I've got to talk to you about.'

'Go on then, twist my arm.' Peters drained his pint and handed her the glass. The storm that had been threatening since mid afternoon was hitting the windows. 'Don't fancy going out in that lot, anyway.'

Rain hit and sheeted down the car's windscreen giving a watery visibility even without the wipers.

'What do you reckon, Wendy?' D.I. Wainwright hit the button once and cleared the view of the darkened house.

'Looks like no one's home again.'

'Any contact recently?'

'The guy in charge, what's his name?' She checked her note book by pencil torch. 'Peters, the one you saw when they first got here, was in the pub last night. Said none of them had seen anything. Call came in this afternoon, from the woman – Ms Steadman, something about a note.'

Wainwright reached for the door. 'Right then. Better check it out. I'll just see that there's no one there and then we'll try the pub.' The police radio crackled into life. 'Get that, will you?' he said and dashed from the car.

He was only gone a few minutes but he came back soaked.

'Found this.' He waved a piece of paper at her. 'They're down the pub. What did they want?' he asked, indicating the radio.

'It was Superintendent Moorehouse, Regional Crime Squad,' she said quietly. 'They think they've got him.'

'Got him?' Wainwright's face creased with disbelief. 'Saunders?'

She shook her head. 'Not Saunders. Someone else. Got form apparently. They picked him up locally, for routine questioning, and he confessed.'

'How can they be sure they've got the right one? They'll be confessing in droves to this.'

'He fits the description of someone seen hanging around where she lived. He hasn't got an alibi and there's other stuff connecting him. Moorehouse thinks he's a real prospect, wants you back there as soon as possible.'

'What did Moorehouse say, exactly?' Wainwright asked.

'Tell him to stop effing about in the middle of nowhere, wasting time and resources and get his arse over here. Is what he said exactly.'

If she said it with a smile it was too dark to detect one. He was glad about that because he was beginning to feel all kinds of a fool. He'd been sure it was Saunders and that he would come here, so bloody sure. It was him and he was here somewhere. He felt it in his bones. But how could it be? Disappointment and fatigue sapped at his certainty. They'd had the whole area locked up tight for days and they'd got sod all. No positive sightings, nothing.

'I hope to God they're right, Wendy,' he said as she turned the car round, 'and stop at the first services you get to, I'm starving.'

*

Mike sat, his pint hardly touched, staring morosely in front of him. Liz had just proposed a change of plan, what he termed a 'worse case scenario'. She had been rehearsing what to say all day and the note had clinched it, but it hadn't made it any easier. She thought that they should not go on the bivouac. Tomorrow was the last day of the trip. This was the last trip of the year. The whole course had to be completed by the end of the month. A compulsory part of the course for the Exam group was the bivouac. A night in the open, camping on their own, without cover and without direct supervision. It was designed to test their resourcefulness, their survival techniques. It had all been planned out months ago, but that was before they knew that one of the known hazards would be a killer on the loose. Liz considered that to be too great a test for their survival skills.

'I knew you wouldn't like it,' she said eventually. 'But I don't see that we have any choice. We just can't take the risk.'

'Come on, Liz. You know how important this is. If we don't go, they fail, and that's that. We haven't got another chance.'

'I know that but maybe we can write to the Exam Board or something.' She leaned towards him. 'There's a murderer out there. We can't leave a bunch of kids on their own, all night, in the middle of nowhere.'

'Rubbish!' Mike Peters tried to control his anger. 'He could be anywhere! We've only got that copper's word for it, and they don't know anything. Police know bugger all if you ask me. Talk about overreacting!'

'What about the note?'

'What about it?' Peters flattened it on the table. 'The police haven't been back to you about it, have they? On its own it doesn't prove anything.'

116

'It does, Mike. It proves . . .' Liz looked at the note again, not quite sure now. In the bright pub with all the noise and people, what did it prove? And it was true the police had not been back to her. She opened her mouth to say something else and then stopped. He thought she was being hysterical already. He'd think she'd freaked out entirely if she told him about that.

'Look, Liz,' he waved his hand in front of her worried stare, 'why don't you phone them? Phone the police from here if it will put your mind at rest.'

'OK. Yeah.' She got up smiling and sorted through the coins on the table for change. 'Good idea.'

'What did they say?' he asked when she came back.

'Well, I spoke to a local bloke. He said that we were scheduled for a visit but that since then they had received new information and the focus of the investigation had shifted elsewhere. Said not to worry about it.'

She folded up the note and shoved it back in her pocket, some of the concern leaving her face.

He grinned broadly. 'There you are, you see? Told you it was all a fuss about nothing. We can carry on as normal now, can't we?'

Chapter 19

Good Morning! It's eight-thirty this Tuesday
morning with another heat wave day across the UK!
It's gotta be some kind of record! We're checking in
the studio – phone or fax us if *you* know. Now it's
time for the news from across the nation. Stay tuned
to Radio One!

The DJ's light slick voice was replaced by the well-
modulated tones of a BBC news reader.

Police reported late last night that they are holding a
man for questioning in connection with the murder
of teenager, Angela Bingham. Sixteen-year-old
Angela, whose body was found on Saturday, is
thought to have been sexually assaulted and to have
died from multiple stab wounds.

All over the house people stopped, frozen in what they
were doing. Chris turned the hair dryer off at the mains.
Anna still held the silent muzzle to her head. Chris knelt
on the floor and studied the radio as if there was a little
person in there who would come out and tell her some
more.

'Yeah! Well! That's all right!' Anna shouted, her eyebrows lifting from their listening frown. 'What a relief!
Maybe we can all get back to normal now, instead of
jumping at our own shadows. God, Chris. You know the

other night in Diane's room? They even got me at it. When we heard that noise and Natalie screaming, I've never been so scared in my whole life. Turn it back on, will you? Hey,' she shouted over the whine of the drier, 'who do you reckon left that note you found yesterday?'

'I don't know,' Chris mumbled. 'Probably someone pratting around.'

'Yes,' Anna agreed. 'That's what I was thinking. Probably Gary or someone stupid like that. Anyway, it doesn't matter now, does it?'

'No, I don't suppose it does.' Chris grinned with relief.

Anna turned the hair drier off.

'You know the business with Andy? Do you still feel the same?'

The grin faded from Chris's face.

'Yes,' she said, 'I still feel the same.'

Liz Steadman looked down at herself, decided the T-shirt was big enough to cover most things, and went to meet the hammering at her door.

'Yeah? What is it? Oh, hi, Mike.'

Mike Peters stood in front of her in a pair of football shorts. They looked each other up and down. Liz smiled, you had to hand it to the PE boys, they kept themselves in good shape.

'Did you hear on the radio? Can I come in?'

'Dressed like that?' She stared pointedly at the curling hair round his navel. 'You've got to be joking! Be all around the place in a minute. I can't afford the scandal.'

'OK.' He pulled his shorts down a bit and then back up. 'But now it's official and we ought to talk about it.'

'Yes, I know.' She grinned at him. 'I was only kidding,

come in. I was just making some coffee, do you want some?'

'Yeah, sure. Be great.'

Liz was glad of an excuse to turn away from him. She did not yet feel in control of the mixture of emotions that were sweeping over her. Ever since their first day here they had been living with the terrifying possibility that a proven killer was closing in on them. The phone call last night had done little to put her mind at rest. Fear had become like a physical presence. Having to confront it in herself, having to control it in so many people, to stop it blowing up into mass hysteria, had wound her up like a spring, bringing her as near as she had ever come to breaking point. And all the time he had been hundreds of miles away. When she had heard that she hadn't known whether to laugh or cry.

'No milk, I'm afraid,' she said. 'Sugar?'

'Don't use it,' he said, stirring in the milk substitute. 'It's all systems go then. You know what I always thought about this killer-on-the-loose business, I always said it was a load of bollocks.'

'Yeah, I guess so. Just goes to show you were right all the time, Mike.'

He regarded her suspiciously as she smiled at him. She felt the sort of euphoria people must feel when they had been right in the path of a hurricane and it had suddenly been diverted.

'Great. I'll tell them the bivvy's on then.'

'Hang on a minute,' she said, suddenly serious. 'Don't you think we ought to wait for some sort of official confirmation that they really have got the right guy?'

'What more confirmation do you want, Liz?' he sighed with exasperation. 'They told you last night, more or less

120

and now you've just heard it on the national news. They don't put out stuff like that unless they're absolutely certain.'

'Yes, I know. All right. What are we going to do for the rest of the day?'

'Well, I was thinking I might take a group white water canoeing.'

Liz regarded him levelly. Not all of them, of course. Not Colin and Natalie for a start, useless pair of fat puppies. Not Chris O'Neill after yesterday's performance. Definitely not Diane. No way. She was trouble, Mike didn't like girls like her. He'd leave Anna if he could and just take the lads, except Anna was the best canoeist of the lot.

'All right.' She shrugged. 'I'll look after the rejects.'

'Magic, Liz!' He drained his coffee. 'Owe you one! Thanks for the coffee. Got to run.'

He was out of his seat and gone. She sat down again and drank her coffee slowly. She didn't have to hurry now. She had all day. She could hear him running around the house, giving orders. Waves of relief broke over her, leaving her feeling drained and weak. They could carry on as normal now. There's no reason not to, was there? It would be all right now there were only the usual things to go wrong. Now that the shadowy figure, who had cast such fear over their time here, was gone.

'You OK up there?' Mark shouted up to Anna, who was checking that the top level of canoes was secure in the trailer.

'Yeah, I got it. That's the last one.'

She jumped down. He caught her and held her just a

second too long. He felt the shiver run through her long muscular body in the moment before she moved out of his arms.

'Look, Mark.' She looked up at him. He was surprised to see that she was blushing, surprised at how serious she was. 'I really like you but . . .'

He laughed softly and brushed her hair out of the way so that he could see into her eyes.

'It's OK, Anna, it's no problem. I like you too, you know, I like you a lot.'

'It's just that at the moment, I'm just not ready for anything.' Her voice tailed off in confusion but her eyes said she didn't want to hurt him, they spoke of her doubt and trouble better than the words she was trying to say.

He touched his finger to her lips and smiled down at her. 'Like I said, it's OK.'

The closeness lasted for only a moment. Then they moved away from each other back into their own separate space.

Chris stood at the upstairs window, watching them, wondering what they were laughing and whispering about. As if she didn't know. Last night when they got back from the pub, she couldn't explain how she felt about Andy or why she had decided to finish with him, it was too complicated, but she knew that she couldn't go out with him any more. She had asked Anna to take him a note.

'I don't believe you are making me do this!' Anna had stared at her in disbelief.

'Please, Anna!' she found herself saying. 'I can't! If he's not there – give it to Mark, or someone.'

'But why?'

Anna's dark eyes searched hers. Chris bowed her head, she would not let Anna see her face.

'OK, give it to me.' She held out her hand and Chris wordlessly gave her the note. She straightened out the shape of Chris's fingers, the 'Y' smudged across the envelope. 'You shouldn't do it like this, though. It's not fair.'

'I know it isn't! But just do it, Anna.' Chris was desperate now. 'Do it for me.'

'All right, all right.' Anna had reluctantly agreed. 'I don't like it. But I'll do it.'

This morning she had heard nothing from Andy, not directly, but when she had gone in for breakfast he had simply got up and walked out. It had been like two freezing cold fronts passing each other. They had ignored each other so totally that they might as well have been the only ones in the room. They all knew, though. They had all known when it started and they all know now it's over. Weird that, Chris thought. But nobody was saying a thing, not to her anyway. It made her feel different, separate, like when someone had died. It was a lonely feeling.

Peters slammed out of the house and strode towards Mark, Anna and Gary who were standing by the trailer, laughing and talking, enjoying the early morning sun.

'What are you lot doing just hanging about?' he shouted over to them. 'Gary, where are the binoculars? I can't find them anywhere. You had them last.'

'Put them in the front of the bus, Sir!' Gary shouted back.

'Get over there and look for them then!'

Gary shambled off, leaving Anna and Mark on their own. A steady thunk, thunking came from where Andy was loading gear at the back of the bus.

'Steady on, Hendy, mate,' Gary called out to him. 'You'll do yourself a damage!'

Andy's reply was hard, sharp and very much to the point.

'Charming.' Gary scowled as he climbed into the bus.

The loading gained in ferocity.

'Not taking it too well, then?' Anna observed.

'You could say that,' Mark replied, studying his finger nails. 'In fact, you could say he's not taking it too well at all. You could say he was well pissed off about it. The letter's in pieces this big!' He indicated confetti size and grinned. 'He's not used to people saying no. It just doesn't happen to him. Well, not very often, and as for girls?' He spat on the ground and rubbed it away. 'Never. Can't say he hasn't had it coming, though.' He shook his head, creased up with silent laughter. 'Nice one. You can tell her that from me.'

Anna smiled and thought again about how much she really liked Mark. He could act really hard but there was something different about him. He said less and thought more – and with his brains. The idea of him. Anna suddenly realized that she could get used to that.

'No binocs in there, Sir.' Gary emerged blinking into the bright morning sun.

'Are you sure?'

'Yes, Sir. Sure, Sir.' Gary shrugged and started to wander away.

Peters made a strangled, whinnying noise. A little vein throbbed in the side of his head.

'Where are you going now? Come here!'

'What, Sir?' Gary asked as he returned to where Peters was standing.

'Go back in the house and get some more you stupid cretin!'

Peters drove each word home with a sharp jab to the shoulder, pushing Gary backwards. When he was up against the door, Peters pulled him away, yanked it open and shoved him inside.

With Peters in this kind of mood, Anna thought, we're in for a real fun day.

The shouting down there, all the noisy activity, made Chris feel exhausted. This was the last day, thank God. With any luck she would be able to avoid Andy until they were back home. Then they would be able to lose each other in the comfortable familiarity of their separate worlds.

At last Peters leapt up into the bus. He revved it viciously, gravel crunched and spat from the wheels as he took the steep slope of the driveway and choking clouds of blue smoke hung in the still air. Chris felt lightheaded with relief when all she could hear was running water and bird song.

'Mariana at the Moated Grange.'

'Say what?'

'Oh,' Anna laughed, embarrassed, 'that's what she reminded me of, standing there at the window. It's a poem or something. We did it with Anderson last year. It's about this woman waiting in this big house, left there by her lover, she can't escape . . .' Her voice trailed off.

'Was it good?' The bus rattled up the slope and jolted on to the road. Mark braced his legs against the seat in front.

'Yes, it was,' Anna smiled, 'as poems go.'

125

'I'm good at waiting,' Mark said, studying the passing hillside. 'I'll still be here, if you change your mind.'

Anna laughed softly and touched his knee. 'Yeah, I know.'

Andy sat by himself at the back of the bus and watched them. He bit and tore at the skin around his thumbnail. Mark and Anna, having a great crack. A good laugh was it? Well, he'd see about that. But it would have to wait.

He returned to the familiar trackways in his mind. He could not remember when he had really started to notice her, but it was a long time now. It had been like learning a new word, which had always been there but suddenly you saw it all over the place. Chris O'Neill was like that. She had always been around. He just hadn't noticed her. Then, quite suddenly, she was everywhere. She was on his mind all the time. He could think of nothing else. When he had found out that she was coming on this trip, he couldn't believe his luck.

No one would say he lacked bottle, but it had taken courage of a different kind to ask her out. Like making that tape. It had taken so many takes to get it right and he had worried she wouldn't be able to hear his words for his heart beat. But he could not have asked her face to face. When she said yes, it was a feeling he couldn't describe, he had longed for that moment so much.

He had wanted to give her everything. The fact that she might not want it, that she could throw it back at him and flirt with other guys, like those climbers in the pub, was unacceptable to him. She had to understand. He had to make her see. But every minute until tomorrow was accounted for. There would be no time when they could be alone together, when he could tell her how he felt.

Blood oozed into the ragged fissure at the side of his nail, making it smooth and red. He had done everything

126

right and she had put him here in this pain. He had not known that it was possible to feel so numb, and hurt so much at the same time. He had not cried since he was a kid, but he knew that if he started now, he would not be able to stop. He had to do something to stop this pain. Andy had never felt like this before. It was like being pushed into unknown territory. There had to be a way out, had to be, had to be. The words took up the rhythm in his head, the rhythm of the road.

One thing was for sure: there was too much unfinished business between them for Andy to leave things as they were. Suddenly the tension began to ease out of his powerful compact body. He sucked at his mutilated thumb and tasted the blood. Physical pain was easier, he understood that.

Chatter and noise diminished as people settled into the journey. The old bus slowed to take the long curving bend in the steep mountain road and disappeared from view. High on the hill twin points of light flashed, as the binoculars turned back to re-focus on the house, but the face at the window had gone.

Chapter 20

Chris lay in the sun, watching black dots dance in a sea of red and making up conversations in her head. She had flattened a patch of long grass right at the end of the overgrown garden. It was as far away from the house as she could get and she hoped no one would find her here.

'D'you mind if I join you?' Chris didn't say yes, but then she didn't say no, so Diane sat down anyway. 'Brought you a drink. Cold from the fridge.' She shrugged. 'Please yourself. It's here if you want it, I'll put it by your elbow. Want some of this?'

'Some of what?' Chris had to open her eyes to see what Diane was offering.

'I like shocking pink,' Diane was applying a first coat of varnish to her long perfect nails. 'Glad we haven't got to do anything today.' She fanned the fingers of her right hand and regarded them critically. 'All that climbing played havoc with my nails.'

'No, thanks.' Chris hid her fingers and their stubby bitten nails.

Diane's high-cut Lycra swimsuit, the same shade as her nail varnish, glowed against her dark skin. Chris looked down at her own white body, turning pink in last year's wrinkling baggy bikini. Diane's one piece was like a second skin. Chris felt even more depressed.

'Got my own tan, but I like the sun.' Diane closed her eyes and turned her face up to catch the full heat of it.

Chris smiled in spite of herself. 'That's what Anna always says.'

'That right? I just thought she was just naturally dark.'

'No,' Chris shook her head. 'Her Dad's from Guyana or somewhere.'

Neither of them spoke for a long time. Diane was on her second coat before she said:

'You don't have to talk about it if you don't want to.'

'That's fine, then,' Chris mumbled into her arms, 'because I don't want to.'

'Is it true, though?' Diane blew on her nails to dry them.

'Is what true?'

'You know. About you and Andy breaking up.'

Chris sat up and zipped open the can Diane had brought out for her. She knew it was no use playing for time or trying to blank her out. Once Diane was on to something like this she wouldn't give up until she had it all. It was no good asking her not to tell anybody. Talking to Diane about anything was as good as issuing a general bulletin. Chris drank some Coke and watched the little brown bubbles chase around the rim. Maybe that was no bad thing. If she told Di now, she could get it over with. They would all know then and they wouldn't keep on at her about it.

'Yeah, it's true,' she said at last. 'Whatever it was is over now. It's over as far as I'm concerned. We weren't exactly going with each other, anyway.'

'Could have fooled me.' Diane's finely shaped eyebrows arched in disbelief.

Chris blushed and looked away.

Diane started applying the top coat. 'Three coats is better, it doesn't chip so easy.' She blew on the nails she had completed. 'Do you reckon you're being fair to him? Given him a real chance? He's dead keen on you.'

'What's that supposed to mean?' Chris had meant to stay really cool about this, but Diane could find and expose what you most wanted to hide with laser precision. She was an expert at it. 'Is he being fair to me? No one's considering me in all this. What right has he got to impose his feelings on me? I don't know why you're defending him. Look how he's treated you.'

Diane looked up from her nails, straight into Chris's eyes and said: 'I care about him, that's why.'

'Look, I like you, Di. I don't want to fight with you about this. Let's just agree not to talk about it. OK?'

'Yeah, yeah, OK.' Diane flicked her fingers around to dry the paint. 'Oh, no. Look! Horrible black midgy things spoiling the finish. I hate the country.' She held her hand up for Chris to inspect. 'What did he say?'

Chris closed her eyes against Diane's relentless gaze.

'If you must know, he said he loved me but he doesn't know what love is.' Her voice was trembling slightly. 'For that matter, neither do I.'

'I don't know what it is with girls like you, Chris,' Diane said, shaking her head. 'I really don't. You've got all these hunky guys lusting after you and you don't know what to do with them. And you're so miserable! Why do you make it into such a big deal? If it was me, I'd have no problems figuring out what to do.'

'Which "hunky guys" exactly?' Chris asked warily.

'Oh, come on. What have we just been talking about? Andy for one. And Nick Stephens.'

Chris felt guilt hit her like a physical blow, then shame followed like another one. She had not thought about Nick since their first evening here.

'Well,' she said bitterly, 'you ought to know all about him.'

'What's that supposed to mean?'

'Come on, Di. There's no point in pretending now. Who went with him after the disco on Thursday night? He might have taken me home but that's all he did. And it wasn't much compared with what happened later from what I hear.'

'What are you talking about?' Diane asked, genuinely puzzled.

'You and Nick, of course,' Chris said angrily. 'You know what I'm talking about!'

'Me – and Nick! You must be joking!' Diane's high laugh ricocheted round the garden. 'He thinks I'm a right slag. Snobby kid like that? You got to be doing ten GCSEs to get a date with him and I'm Alternative Programme.'

She picked up a daisy, split its stem with her long pink thumbnail and posted a second flower through the sappy gap.

'Come off it, Diane! You went with him. I know!'

'Oh yeah?' Diane cast about coolly for more daisies, amassing a small pile for her chain. 'And how exactly do you know?'

'You were seen.'

'That right? And who saw us?'

'Anna. Anna saw you meeting outside the chip shop. She saw you go with him.'

'That a fact?' Diane said, thoughtfully discarding the last daisy she picked because the stem was too short. 'Then she went rushing off to tell you, I suppose.'

'No, she didn't rush to tell me. She just told me, that's all.'

'Right. I see.' The chain was growing longer. Stubby little daisies swung between Diane's knees. 'And did she also tell you that Nick lives down our end and that we've known each other since we were little kids? And that I might think he's a snobby git and he might think I'm a slaggy cow but we're really good mates. She tell you that?'

'No, of course she didn't,' Chris said impatiently. She didn't like where this was leading to.

'No, of course she didn't. She didn't know that, did she?' Diane shook her head and smiled, full of mock pity and concern. 'You and Anna, everyone thinks you're so clever. You think you're so clever. You know naff all, really.'

Chris found she'd picked a daisy too, and angrily threw it away.

'So let Aunty Di tell you what *really* happened – not what happened in your fevered little imaginations. I'm hanging out with some mates and it's getting late, see? He comes up and says, You walking home? I says, You asking? I'm walking. That's how we are, see?'

Images she had never really noticed were coming back, of them laughing and talking, hanging out together with easy familiarity. She should have known.

'So he walks me home. And that's *all* he does except he's talking about you. How pretty you are and how clever you are and how much he wants to go out with you. He even asks me what I think his chances are. And I say, because I clocked you at the Disco with his tongue half-way down your throat, I say I think they're pretty good. And do you know what?'

'No, what?' Chris rested her head on her hands so she did not have to look at Diane.

'He was over the moon. I mean, well chuffed.'

Diane held up her daisy chain and regarded it critically.

132

It was near completion. At least it was nearly as long as she intended to make it. She carefully chose a few more specimens.

'He's not going to be too chuffed now, is he?'

Chris stared at the ground miserably. The same thought had occurred to her.

'I mean,' Diane carefully linked the first and last flowers together, 'soon as you are out of his sight, you're off with someone else. I've seen some fast work in my time, but I've got to hand it to you, Princess.' She shook out the daisy chain and delicately placed it on Chris's head. 'You win the prize for it.'

Diane got up, brushed herself down and snapped the bottom of her bright pink suit. She found her high-heeled sandals and put them on. Her dark eyes glittered as she looked at Chris over the top of her sunglasses.

'You've really mucked it up this time. Haven't you, sweetheart?' she said. 'Be seeing you.'

Diane blew her a kiss and swung off up the garden. Chris went over what Diane had just told her, feeling even worse now than she had done earlier. If only she had known all that before, it never would have started in the first place, and she would still have stood a chance with Nick.

It was all Anna's fault, jumping to conclusions. What did her father say? Too clever by half. Bloody right. She pulverized the daisies she had been plucking to green slime.

Chapter 21

'Hi! How are you doing?' Anna threw herself down on the grass next to Chris and unlaced her hiking boots. 'Nice day, huh? You been out here all the time? I wish I had.' She started pulling off her shirt. 'It's OK – don't panic. I've got me cossy on under here. Hey, Chris, shift over a bit – I'm on the grass!'

Chris did not move and she did not speak. I'm not going to talk to her, she thought, I'm not going to say anything at all.

'What's the matter? Chrissy?' Anna asked, puzzled. 'Why aren't you talking? It's me. Anna. Friend. Are you upset about something? Is it Andy? Do you want to talk about it? Hey – you better put some of this on, you're burning up!'

Chris felt the cool liquid dabbled on to her shoulders and Anna's fingers spreading it lightly, sliding all over her back.

'No it's not Andy. And I don't want to talk about it. Stop doing that! I can burn if I want to. Go away and leave me alone!'

Chris wriggled furiously from under Anna's hands and turned over to confront her. Anna's grin thinned and her throat tightened. Chris's eyes were clouding up fast, like a storm gathers over the sea. She's really mad about something, Anna thought, and it's something to do with me.

'You lied to me.' Chris's words came small and quiet, edged like knives.

Anna tried to laugh. 'About what?'

'About Nick Stephens and Diane. And don't say you didn't, because I know you did. I've been talking to Diane.'

'I didn't lie to you,' Anna said, trying to keep her voice bright and even. 'What did she tell you?'

Despite her resolution not to talk to Anna it all came spilling out. It added up to the destruction of everything and it was all laid at Anna's door. Anna listened carefully and did not reply immediately. She leaned back on her elbows, chewing on a blade of grass and stared out at the hills.

Finally she spat out the grass and said: 'Look, I'm sorry. I saw them and put two and two together.'

'And came up with a hundred and fifty. Just jumping to conclusions. Typical. No proof, nothing, just straight in there.'

'How was I supposed to know that they've been bosom pals since they were three? Sounds a likely story if you ask me. Bet she was a slag in play group. I thought he was messing you about and I didn't like it.' Anna sat up, hugged her knees and sighed, 'Now tell me what's really the matter.'

'That is what's really the matter. You lied to me.'

Anna stared into Chris's eyes. 'I did not lie to you. I told you what I saw, that's all, and you believed me.'

'Of course I believed you. Why shouldn't I believe you? You're my best friend, aren't you?'

'I'm your best friend,' Anna said quietly, leaning into Chris's anger. 'So tell me what this is all about? And I don't mean Nick Smoothy and this year's winner of the

135

BAFTA Bonking Award. OK – I made a mistake. I got it wrong and I'm sorry.' Anna reached forward, removing the twisted thread of Chris's withered daisy crown. 'Now can you tell me what this is really about?'

Her words were matter of fact but were spoken with the quiet authority and concern that Anna reserved for the most serious discussions that searched the depths of their friendship.

Insects buzzed around her and cut out, like tiny chain saws, while Chris re-assessed the source of her confusion and anger. She had genuinely thought that it was what Anna had said about Nick and Diane, and only that, but Anna was right. She was using that to mask something else which disturbed her far more deeply. She needed time to figure out exactly what it was and how to talk about it.

'It's not just that,' she sighed. 'It's about Andy.'

'About the fight you had last night?'

Chris nodded. 'It sounds petty and everything now but at the time it wasn't. I felt really humiliated. I borrowed some money from Steadman. And then, when I was at the bar, he paid her off. It made me feel really stupid, like a little kid. And I'd *told* him not to buy me anything or pay for anything else. Whatever I say, if he doesn't want to hear it, he just blanks me out. He kept going on about those guys in the pub, looking at me, chatting me up, like I was encouraging them or something. When I try to deny it, he's not even listening. He thinks he owns me.'

'That's what he's like.' Anna closed her eyes and sighed. 'He wants to have you to gloat over, with his Ray-Ban sunglasses and his Reebok trainers.'

Chris wrenched up grass savagely. 'Well, I don't like it.'

'Look, Chris, you've seen him with Elaine. He's all

over her one minute and the next minute he's treating her like shit. Did you see that Valentine card he gave her? "To My Darling Girlfriend", all covered in pink satin hearts and disgusting puppy dogs. Really gross. You're better off out of it.'

'I know, but when I went back to my room this morning, I found this.'

Chris took something from her bag and handed it to Anna half furtively, like it was something she was ashamed of. As Anna accepted the book, the broken lock flipped open and flashed golden in the harsh glare of the afternoon sun.

'It's my diary,' Chris said miserably. 'Anna, he's read my diary! And that bit, where he's written, goes through from now to the end of July. I'll have to tear out half the pages!'

Anna turned the leaves to read the words he had written there.

'Do you think he means it?' Chris asked her eventually.

'Which bit?' Anna asked. 'The part that says "I love you", or the less flattering observations, like you being a real user and a hard bitch?'

'When you took my note, last night, who did you give it to?'

'I gave it to Andy. I told you before, I haven't got time for all that go-between business.'

'I've cocked it up with him and Nick,' Chris said miserably. 'I've made a real mess of this, haven't I?'

'So what?' Anna was finding it hard to conceal her impatience. 'If you want my advice you should cut your losses. You'll only get in deeper. Leave it, Chris.'

'I've got to see him,' Chris was suddenly intense. 'I must talk to him. I . . .' She was interrupted by shouting from near the house.

'Anna? Where are you? We've got to get ready. They'll be going in a minute.'

'That's Michaela,' Anna said, lacing her boots. 'We've got to go. The bivouac's on. That's what I came down here to tell you. There's really no time left, Chris.'

Chapter 22

He put the binoculars down and lit a cigarette, carefully snapping the match and putting it in his pocket. Someone had taught him to do that, but he could not remember when or why. Sometimes his mind was moving fragments: an imploding TV screen on an imploding TV screen. Some parts were disappearing in on themselves; others flew out and away, bright shiny jagged-edged pieces going end over end, into infinity. When he had first felt this happening it had frightened him. Now he hardly noticed. He saw only the bright surfaces of things, recognizing them but seeing also, as if for the first time, the colour of a cigarette packet, the wording on a chocolate bar. Some of the things from inside his head he saw flashing by, others he could not find. He had not forgotten them. They were just not there any more. They had gone, been lost. Maybe for a short time. Maybe for ever.

Sometimes, like now, a video played in real time and he saw a portion of his life being acted out before him. He was looking down at the big house, but he did not see now what he had been studying a minute ago, those two girls stretched out in the garden. He saw everything how it was years ago. The drive was not rutted and scarred now, but was smooth, with rake lines in the gravel. The windows of the house shone in spring sunshine. A woman in a pink overall hung clothes on a line. The garden was immaculate, its knife-edged borders full of spring flowers. Daffodils, primulas and auriculas, he could remember all their names. Gwyn liked a good display early on to show that old winter had really gone, and it was easily the best in the neighbourhood. He could see himself down there in the vegetable patch, helping to plant out brassicas. Sometimes it was like this, when you could see yourself in a dream, other times it was as if you were looking out from inside your own skin. His younger self was suddenly closer. He could see himself, skinny and small, in ill-fitting clothes, worn thin from other people's wearing. He had not had anything brand-new, just worn by him, until he was a teenager and had nicked it himself. He could feel the wet grainy soil between his fingers, under his nails. He stared down at his clean hands with unseeing eyes.

He'd spent a lot of time in that garden helping Gwyn, because he didn't get on well with the other boys. Gwyn looked after the garden and grounds while his wife, Bet, did the cooking and housekeeping. They had both been good to him. He knew why he had come to this place, well, most of the time. He knew what they had told him. Something very bad had happened to him, something so bad it meant he could never live with his own parents. He had not discovered whether the bad thing was something they had done to him or whether it was something he had done; but in his own mind it came down to the same thing – they did not want him. This was a place for kids like him. Kids nobody wanted. A place where they could live and be looked after and a place where they would be safe. The chances that they might also be happy were pretty remote. But Gwyn and Bet had made him happy, for a little while. It was the only place where he had known some sort of peace.

He stood up and stretched, bones and sinews cracking. He had let it go on for too long and all his plans to get

140

them out had come to nothing. Time was running out. He had to decide now what to do, things could not go on like this. I won't be needing those any more, he thought, and dropped the binoculars over the edge of the cliff.

Chapter 23

The bivouac group were late going out to their overnight camp. Chris had watched them straggling up into the hills in a ragged column, Peters chivvying at them like a German shepherd dog. Anna and Mark were walking together with Michaela scurrying along behind. At the last minute Diane had elected to go too. Chris grinned to herself. Some people would go to any lengths and that's a fact. She must have reckoned she had a chance now Chris was out of the frame, but she was struggling to keep up with Michaela. She would never catch Andy way out in front. They disappeared out of sight as the last of the sunlight left the highest tops of the bald hills.

Down here in the valley dusk was deepening to darkness. Chris shivered and wished that someone would press a button and beam her home, away from this place where one source of tension was just replaced by another. The whole experience had become a lengthening ordeal, a series of tests which had left her exhausted and that she knew she had failed. Even if they could, even when she was home for good, things were not necessarily going to be the same, were they? Nick would be there, for a start, waiting for her. Where would that leave Andy? His not being there tonight was a temporary respite and she knew it. She would have to see him, she owed him that much.

Things had happened here that could not easily be undone.

She turned on her Walkman, tuning into a music station, seeking for distraction from her circling thoughts. It took several seconds for the newsflash to penetrate but she heard it out, holding the headset to her ears like a radio operator and stumbling to her feet. She covered the distance to the house with the speed of an athlete.

Natalie looked up from the Scrabble board she was setting up as Chris crashed into the common room.

'Ah, there you are,' she smiled. 'D'you want a game?'

Chris shook her head impatiently. 'Where's Steadman? It's urgent. I've got to find her.'

'In her room, I think. What's it about, Chris?'

'Can't stop now,' Chris was already out of the door. 'I'll tell you later.'

Chris burst into Ms Steadman's room without knocking.

'Have you got a radio in here?' She gasped. 'Quick. Turn it on.'

Liz Steadman took one look at her and did as Chris said. The blood drained from her face as they listened to the News.

. . . O'Clock News. The man being held in connection with the death of Angela Bingham has been released from custody. Police hunting Angela's killer are now extremely anxious to contact Clive Alan Saunders. Saunders is described as being about five foot eight inches tall with dark hair, light-coloured eyes and a pale, pasty complexion. He is thought to be in the North Wales area. A police statement, issued late this afternoon, describes him as potentially very dangerous and warns members of

143

the public not to approach him. Anyone with any information as to his whereabouts should contact the police immediately.

'The bivouac party!' Chris shouted over the rest of the bulletin. 'We've got to stop them.'

'It's too late, Chris.' Ms Steadman turned the radio off. 'They've gone. There aren't any roads up where they're heading and I'm not even sure which route they've taken.'

'Ms Steadman,' Chris started. 'I think I know who he is.' She told her of Gary's suspicions about the policeman who wasn't a policeman, the same man she'd seen at the fairground, the one that must have left the note.

'I know.' Ms Steadman nodded slowly. 'That had crossed my mind too.'

'I should have said something, but,' she paused, feeling awkward, 'after the news this morning, I thought I was just imagining things, being stupid, and anyway, I couldn't see how he was getting in and out.'

'I know the feeling,' Ms Steadman confessed uneasily. 'Yesterday I was sure someone had been in here, in this room. But I thought I was just being paranoid. I dismissed it. It didn't seem possible.' She glanced round. 'It was locked, you see.'

Chris searched the room while Ms Steadman was speaking, trying to see it in a different way, looking for some clue. Then she saw it. It was so simple, it was terrifying. The panels at the far end of the room were not windows at all. They were doors, half glass, half panelling. She went over to them and saw plainly now what they had failed to notice before. There was a handle half-way up, painted the same colour as the frame. Her eyes followed the line of a flimsy seal of paint that had recently been broken. The bolts at the top, bound down by layers of paint, were disengaged.

'This is how he is getting in, Ms Steadman,' she said quietly. 'Look.' She tried the handle and the doors swung open, cool air billowed the curtains into the room. 'These are french windows. *All* doors and windows. That is what he meant. These have been open all day and all night since we got here.'

Only a slight tremor in her voice betrayed the terror she felt. Liz slowly came over to her. They stood together for a moment as the implications of Chris's discovery sank into them. Then Liz reached around her and pulled the window closed. She stretched up to ram home the paint-stiffened bolts and turned Chris round.

'But we know now, Chris, don't we?' She held the girl by her shoulders, looking into her eyes. 'He won't be able to get in again. It's time we did something about this whole business, instead of sitting around paralysed.'

'What can we do?' Chris's words were barely audible as she followed Liz back to the desk on the other side of the room.

'Get hold of the police for a start off and get them down here. I'm going to sort this out once and for all. Give me the number will you?' she said as she reached for the phone. 'It's on that pad right next to you.'

'What about the bivouac people, Ms Steadman?' Chris could not keep the panic out of her voice. 'They are out there all alone.'

Ms Steadman's hand froze on the telephone and they both stared at it stupidly as the clanging started up and went on, loud and discordant. Neither of them had ever heard the sound before, someone was ringing the big bell that hung outside the front door of the house.

Chapter 24

Chris turned out the light. She was tired, desperate for sleep, but his face kept coming back like an afterimage. She could not get it out of her head.

The man at the door was Detective Inspector Wainwright. Natalie let him in. He explained briefly why he was there and, as they produced the note and told him their story, he paced around, running his fingers down the broken film of paint, trying the bolts, checking the room. After they finished he showed them a strip of photographs. These had recently come into police possession, he explained, and they were believed to be of Clive Alan Saunders.

Is this the man you saw? she heard him say again. Are you sure?

The photos were like you'd get from a booth, passport size, one on top of the other, with no changes of expression from first to last. She had known him straight away but she had studied them carefully, swallowing to get the fear back down her throat. Yes, she recognized him. She had spoken to him outside the house on the first day and seen him later at the fair. She was certain of it.

The policeman looked to Ms Steadman. She nodded her confirmation. It was the same man.

'You know what this means?' he said.

Chris watched, side-lined, as they stared at each other. They suddenly both looked older, white faces tightening, scored by lines of worry and tension, as they weighed up the implications and gathered in the possibilities. Steadman, arms folded, started uttering accusations. The policeman muttered apologies, seeking to reassure.

Then, to Chris's relief, they turned their attention to the whereabouts of the bivouac group. Steadman moved over to the big wall map of the area, indicating their probable destination, he reached for the phone to alert mountain rescue. Chris was dismissed, told to join the rest of the pupils in the common room and given strict instructions not to tell anyone about what had happened. Later she had been sent to bed, along with the others, without learning anything more.

She was wide awake now. It was the only way she knew to fight the long ago dread that had crept in with the darkness, chilling her heart. Her fear of heights would always be with her, nothing could make it less. Her fear of the dark was different. It went back to the witch who had lived under the wardrobe when she was a little girl. With the light out and the door shut, the witch crawled out, swelling up to fill the room. She had lain there for years, waiting for opportunities, until Chris's brother had reached under the wardrobe and retrieved a green glass bead which glittered sometimes in the landing light. It had dwindled and declined after that, until each night-time shape equated with some daytime object, and the room contained no more fear and mystery in the darkness than it did in day.

The old familiar horror stretched across the years to reclaim her. She should have felt safe. There was a policeman downstairs, talking to Steadman, and another one checking the grounds. She could not ask to go in with someone else now. Ms Steadman had enough on her plate without Chris making a fuss about the dark. She would have to sleep alone. She lay with her heartbeat tripping and thudding through the bed, the dread welling in her throat like physical sickness. The strands that she had just plucked from her memory would join the threads of fear that webbed this house, weaving themselves into the fabric of her dreams, and terror would hold her there, wrapped and paralysed, in its strait-jacket.

She was in Steadman's room working in the pool of the desk light, the rest of the room in darkness. The killer was there in the room with her but if she ignored his presence he would leave her alone. She saw herself get up from the desk and walk to the door with infinite casual slowness. Then she was running, faster than she knew she could, up spiralling stairs, along endless shadowed corridors. Finally she reached a room she knew to be a place of safety.

She flung open the door and stepped in but immediately the room seemed to grow and change. When she reached behind her, the door had vanished, her fingers met cold rough stone. She looked around and could see nothing. The darkness seemed complete, suffocating, but at the far end of the room weak grey light filtered through long glass panes. She began feeling her way towards it. Just as she got to the window and reached up to open it, she heard him get out of his chair. He had been waiting for her and he was in no hurry now he had her there. The catch snapped off in her hands as she wrenched it towards her and then, above her shoulder, she saw his reflected face. Dark hair hung in bars over eyes that seemed all black pupil and a thin grin showed red against whitish skin as he lowered his head. His breath touched her neck and stirred her hair as he softly whispered words she could not understand. The killer held her from behind, pinned and helpless, as his face dissolved and re-formed on the other side of the opening window. His arms reached out to embrace her as he stepped inside.

She jerked from sleep, the terror of the dream crushing her chest, her breath coming in shallow gasps as though it was being squeezed out of her. She looked around, waiting for the power of the dream to diminish and for the room to lose its menace now that she was awake. But this did not happen. The little hairs rose on the back of her neck. Fresh sweat broke out around her hairline and sheened her upper lip. He was still there, his dark shape clearly outlined against the grey of the window, his sibilant whisper louder than shouting as he moved across the room.

'Don't scream. Don't shout. Please. I just want to talk to you. I had to come back. I couldn't stay away. I couldn't stop thinking about you. It was driving me crazy. I had to see you, talk to you,' – his whispering was fierce, hypnotic in her head – 'to make you see. I can't live without you. I love you. Chrissy, please!'

'Andy? Oh, thank God it's you! I was having this terrible dream.'

Her words dissolved into helpless sobbing and she clung to him.

'Shh, Shh. It's all right, I'm here now.' He brushed the damp curls back and kissed her forehead. 'I'll look after you.'

He kissed her closed eyes and tasted the wetness of her cheeks. Her mouth was warm and salty, yielding to his. He meant to be gentle, but her helplessness, the way she so desperately clung to him, triggered some deep need inside until there was only desire and its fulfilment. All control went from him.

Words of love and comfort, terms of endearment, were

149

not meant to be expressed like this. She slowly woke up to the terrible difference between what he was saying and what he was doing. She struggled out from under him.

'Andy! For Christ's sake! What do you think you are doing? No, Andy. No! Get off me!'

Her words were cut off. His mouth was heavy on hers, bruising her lips. She felt the corner of a front tooth chip away, and then his tongue deep in her mouth. He forced her back and knelt over her, holding her down. He was so heavy and strong. She had not imagined that he was as strong as this.

She knew that she should fight and struggle. She knew that by doing nothing, she was giving her permission for this to happen; that is how he would see it, how others would see it, how she saw it herself. But she could not will herself to move, it was as though she was in the last part of the dream but could not wake up. Then it was as if she had moved outside herself, as if she had migrated to the ceiling to watch their struggling rhythmic movement.

When it was all over, she felt nothing at all.

He left without saying a word. She lay for a long time, staring up at the dim glimmer of the ceiling, wondering about what had happened to her. There was something in her mouth, like grit. She spat out a tiny white triangle of tooth. Should I keep it, she thought, as some sort of souvenir or trophy? She had an urge to put it under the pillow to see if some adult version of the tooth fairy would come and leave her some appropriate award to mark her passage into womanhood. Her hand closed around the fragment and she curled herself up. Her body was bruised and aching, for in his clumsy urgency he had been rough.

Chapter 25

High up on the hillside above her Clive Alan Saunders was coming to the end of his brooding vigil, preparing to give it up. He turned away from the house and lay looking up at the night sky. He used to lie up here all the time when he was a kid, on any good clear night, staring out and out, seeking individual stars. He never knew their names. He took no interest in that. He made up his own constellations: 'The Gun', 'The Dagger', 'The Prayer'. They were all still there, waiting for him. They seemed so bright and so near, like they could rain down on him and he could hold them in his hands. It was as if he was actually in space. A billion stars showed up like bright metal dust amongst the scattered points of light, and beyond them were billions more, stretching on and on. The constellations began to rotate and he had to close his eyes.

The night sky was immediately replaced. He was back under the heavy oak vaulting of the church roof. The fresh keen air and the clean smell of the high hills went. Last Friday had been the hottest April day for many years. Stale left over air scarfed his nose and mouth. The smell of ancient incense and decaying flowers made him gag. Sweat broke out again under his arms and down his back. She shouldn't have run from him.

The church was in less than half light. He did not know where the lights were. He had to search. It did not take him long to find her. He followed the little scuffling noises and, outside the Vestry door, he paused. In the suffocating silence he heard her rapid breathing and a funny sound, coming from far back in her throat, like an animal might make. He did not like her being afraid of him like that. It was kind of insulting and not part of their relationship. It was not right at all.

When he found her she was trying to get out, trying to force back the heavy rusted bolts on the Vestry door. Her fingernails were torn and bloody. She cradled one hand like a wounded paw. He had not known about that door, but it did not matter. It was futile, futile of her to think that she could escape. And what for? He only wanted to talk to her, after all.

She had not wanted to talk to him. She had shouted and screamed at him, fighting like a wild cat, using words that meant she didn't love him, that she would never love him. It hurt him so much he'd wanted to cry and then it made him angry. He hadn't wanted to do that to her but she made him so mad. And afterwards, she had said she would tell, that she knew who he was and she would tell everybody what he had done. He had got so frightened. Because he couldn't let that happen. He had to shut her up then, didn't he?

He didn't remember much after that. Just coming to and finding her lying there. There had been so much blood. He would never have imagined there could be so much. He had to use some of those cassock things to try and mop it up, he didn't want to leave things in a mess. Some of it had got on him as well. He had sat there for a long time then, wondering what was best to do for her, until the birds and the light told him it was too late to do anything and he'd had to leave.

The knife blade gleamed in the moonlight. Perhaps he had always meant to do that to her. But no, he really

152

didn't think so. It had just happened, kind of an accident. That could happen, when things went wrong, got out of control. It had not been his fault.

He turned over on to his side and rolled up into a ball. He had come here, for this place was magic to him, to forget, to put things back into place. But he couldn't do it. All the times before it had worked, but this was different. Down round the house now activity was growing. He had seen headlights turning into the driveway, soon those torch beams would be ranging up into the hills for him. In the stillness he thought he could hear a helicopter, its rotary blades thrumming, coming to turn night into day and search for him. They would do everything they could now to catch him, but they were already too late.

He looked at the big moon, sectioned by the mountains. Stunted trees and rocky outcrops stood in the serrated silhouette against its silvery surface. The features and contours on the face of the moon were clearer to him than those on the hills opposite. He smeared the tears across his cheeks. He wished he could step on to that clean black and silver world and live there, leaving this lesser place with its shit and filth and blood.

Blood looked black at night. There was just the smell of it, no colour. It flowed out of him now, thin and fast, branching into little streams until it caught and pooled somewhere. The pools filled and rippled with each pumping pulse until they lay hardly moving. He stared on at the silver disc of the moon. It seemed very near. Just a step away. This time he would get there, free and clear.

Chapter 26

The bivouac group's temporary encampment was on a barren windswept plateau, only accessible on foot or horseback. Anna didn't mind that, the bleak isolation didn't bother her. She hadn't minded the tough hike to get there, either. She judged that they hadn't really gone all that far in miles, but it had been quite hard going in the dark. Although it had been a fair climb up to the plateau and their packs were heavy, Anna would have happily carried on walking all night. The part she hated was when Peters told them to disperse and find a suitable camp-site.

Finding somewhere was easy. It was putting up the shelter that was difficult. After half an hour, Anna was nearly crying with frustration. Whatever she tried, she just could not get the bloody thing right. The plastic sheeting, from which she was supposed to make her shelter, tore all over the place. She watched it fluttering about in the tugging wind like a tattered flag on a broken stick. It was cold now. It would be freezing later without a proper shelter. Where the bloody hell had Michaela got to? She had been depending on Michaela to do this stuff. She was a proper little homemaker, but she'd gone off to baby-mind Diane who should never have come in the first place.

At the scrape of a boot and the slither of rockfall behind her, she turned round, snarling, 'Where the hell have you been? You better not have used up all the plastic sheeting.' She stopped when she saw it was Mark and hoped it was too dark for him to see her blushing. 'Oh, it's you. I thought it was Michaela. Sorry.'

Mark flicked his torch over the mess of sticks and plastic in front of her.

'Made a real dog's breakfast of that, haven't you?' he said, grinning. 'Camp craft is not your strong point, Anna, let's face it. When Peters sees that you'll get zilch.'

'I know that! What do you think I'm so pissed off about? Don't just stand there grinning, help me!'

'Hang on a minute.' He flashed his torch round, surveying the whole area carefully. 'You chose a rubbish place for a start off. Look over there, that'd be much better.' His torch illuminated a little coomb to the right of where she stood. 'It's not damp and this thick short grass is nice and soft. You can anchor the bivvy here and here and fix it at the bottom with some rocks. Come on. Cut some bracken. Soon have you dead cosy.'

Anna took out her Swiss army knife and got to work obediently. She'd amassed quite a pile when he said:

'Look!'

'Wow! It's like a real little tent. It's got flaps and everything. You're a genius, Mark.' She threw her arms round his neck, kissing him. 'Thank you.'

'That's OK,' he said, the blood beating in his face as he released himself, 'it's nothing.'

'It is,' she said, 'you saved my life.'

'No. You did that.'

She had to turn away. 'We agreed not to talk about that. Remember?'

'Yes, I remember.' He said it so quietly she could hardly hear him.

Anna started to shiver. 'Oh God, it's getting really freezing.'

155

'Here, have some of this.'

She took a swig, closing her eyes for a second, feeling the quick rush as the spirit hit.

'Oh yeah, that's better.' She took another gulp and handed it back. He drank some himself and replaced the cap.

'I know,' he said, 'let's build a fire.'

'Mark, we're not allowed . . .'

But he was already collecting twigs and dead bracken. Anna watched him break branches off a gnarled tree, dwarfed and bent by the wind, and carefully construct a small hearth out of stones. He was so neat and careful. You'd expect clumsiness from someone who was so big and had such big hands. Anything practical, she thought, and he did it perfectly. Since Mark had appeared she hadn't thought about Chris and Andy or anybody. All the edgy tension that had knotted her up through this nightmare trip had left her, and for the first time in a long time she was enjoying herself. Actually having fun. She laughed out loud. She couldn't remember the last time she'd felt this happy.

'There you go. Brilliant.' Flames flared up and then died down to give out a steady glow. 'What's so funny?'

'Nothing.' She moved close to the fire, enjoying the heat, her smile widening and widening, as though it would never leave her face.

'You should smile more, Anna,' he said, gazing at her, 'no, I'm serious. When you smile like that you look really,' he hesitated before saying it, 'beautiful.'

'Where's Andy, anyway?' She allowed her hair to fall forward, like a veil, not wanting to show what she was feeling.

'I don't know. Pissed off on his own somewhere.'

156

'Never mind.' Anna laughed and put her arm round him. 'You've got me now, haven't you?'

Mark coiled strands of her hair round his finger.

'Have I?' he said.

He pushed the heavy curtain of hair away from her face and their eyes met. Suddenly her throat felt tight and her heart seemed to plummet down inside her.

'Yes,' she murmured, 'if you want.'

His arms went around her but he held her like she was something precious that he was afraid to break. He smelt of cold air and woodsmoke. His mouth was warm. As he kissed her lightly, once, twice, tantalizingly gentle and soft, the image of Paul, that always seemed to be watching her in cold mockery, had faded away like an old Polaroid photograph. The ice glaze layers, that she had thought would hold her for ever, started to craze and melt.

Chapter 27

When the bivouac group were brought back from their expedition some of them were close to complete exhaustion. Anna moved with the same zombie slowness as the others but she wasn't dreaming of sleep and a warm bed. She was thinking over what she was going to tell Chris. She was always saying Anna never shared anything, always accusing her of being a tight mouth. Anna smiled, after tonight she wouldn't be able to say that.

Their room was in darkness. Anna hesitated for a moment and then flipped the light switch. Chris was bound to wake up anyway. There was so much gear, Anna couldn't manage it in the dark and if she left it outside someone would nick it. And she wouldn't mind being woken up, not when she heard what Anna had to tell her.

'Are you awake?' she asked, but Chris made no indication that she'd heard the question. 'You won't believe what's happened.'

She unzipped her coat and stripped it off. There was still no response but, as Anna unlaced her boots, she started telling her about what had happened with Mark anyway. Not every little detail, just the gist of it.

'And then, guess what?'

Anna looked over at the inert body huddled in the duvet and sighed with frustration. What was the point? This was exactly why she didn't bother sharing things. Even if you tried to tell someone how it had been and how you felt, you could never find the right words to tell it. And even if you did, the chances were that, just like now, they weren't even listening.

'We got busted! Just when it was getting interesting. All of a sudden these guys appear and round us all up on police orders, saying we've got to come back. Chris. Chris!' Anna went over to the bed and looked down at her. 'What's happened?' She took Chris by the shoulder, turning her over so that she could see her face. 'Chris?'

Her eyes were puffed almost shut and all round them the skin was blotched red. Fresh tears seeped from the corners and ran down the side of her face.

'Nothing,' Chris said, her voice croaky and slurring through swollen lips.

Anna walked to the bathroom, her heart thudding and her mind racing. What on earth had happened to make her cry like this? She filled a glass with water and rinsed a flannel under the cold tap. She went back and sat Chris up, holding the glass for her to drink, and then she gently washed her face. Chris held the torn edges of her night shirt tightly together. Anna pulled her sweatshirt over her head.

'Here,' she said, 'have this.'

She accepted it without speaking and put it on. The fleeced lining still held the heat of Anna's body but it did not seem to warm her or keep her teeth from chattering. Anna put her arm round her and rubbed her back.

'What's the matter, Chrissy? You've got to tell me. Something must have happened, you've got to tell me what it is.'

'I can't tell you.' Chris's voice was so small Anna could hardly hear her.

'Yes you can,' Anna insisted gently. She touched the damp curls that strayed on to Chris's face and smiled into her tear filled eyes. 'It's me you're talking to. You can tell me what happened.'

Anna held her for a long time. Tears soaked her T-shirt as Chris sobbed out the story and Anna fitted the pieces together. She stroked the fine hair at the back of Chris's head and tried to make her own voice soft and soothing. It was a struggle. Her own eyes burned with tears of anger and outrage. She felt that she could quite easily kill him, without the slightest guilt or regret. She didn't want Chris to see that written on her face.

When the sobbing had subsided into gulps and snuffles she leaned over and reached for a box of tissues.

'Here. Have a good blow,' she said.

Chris blew her nose and sat up.

'Thanks.'

'Best to cry it out. That's what my Nan always says.'

Neither of them could manage a smile.

Chris blew her nose again. 'I feel better now.' She looked around as though she was not quite sure where she was. 'I think I'll take a shower.'

'You shouldn't, you know.' Anna held her arm. 'You shouldn't have a shower. It'll wash away the evidence.'

'What do you mean?'

'What I mean is, what happened to you is rape. You should go right now and report it to Steadman, to the police. It is, Chris!' Anna strengthened her grip to stop her from breaking away. 'What he did to you, it's wrong.'

'No! No! Anna, I can't! You mustn't! You've got to promise me right now,' Chris's eyes filled with agonized pleading as she met Anna's implacable dark gaze, 'you won't tell anyone. Not now. Not ever! Promise me!'

'That's not right,' Anna was shaking her head. 'He shouldn't be allowed to get away with it. It's a crime!'

160

'No, it wasn't,' Chris said, frantic now. 'Not really. I mean, I . . .'

'You didn't want him to do it. Did you?'

'No. But I didn't . . .'

'Didn't what? Fight him off? Scream and shout so everyone came running? So what? You didn't want him to and he went ahead anyway. Then it is.'

'No. It's not as simple as that.' Chris buried her face in her hands.

'What? You led him on? It's your fault for making him want to? Don't be stupid, Chrissy. You mustn't think like that. It is very simple. He did it. He should pay.'

'I know what you're saying is right. But . . .'

Chris shook her head to clear the chaos of thought and feeling which threatened to overwhelm her. She knew she couldn't explain the revulsion and loathing, the deep horror she felt. She knew that she shouldn't feel this way about herself, but she did. Anna's anger was all directed out, towards him. Hers poured down inside her like poison rain. The thought of telling it all to Ms Steadman, to strangers, to her parents. The thought of them knowing, assessing and appraising her and then their eyes reflecting back what she thought about herself. She just could not do it. It would spread and spread, like a stain. Everyone would know. They would talk behind her back, nudging and smirking or being kind and pitying. She couldn't bear any of that.

'I'm not going to do anything about it,' she said finally. 'So you are not to either. Anna, give me your word.'

She searched her friend's face. There was little reassurance. Deep frown lines drew Anna's brows together in a thick bar over eyes that burned deep with hatred. Her full mouth curved down in sullen anger, under her dark gold complexion she was livid. A muscle jumped in her cheek. Her whole face was setting into savage determination. When she was like this, Chris knew, she was capable of anything and nothing would stop her.

'Anna listen to me, please! It wasn't like that, not strictly speaking. I thought to begin with, when I knew there was somebody in the room, that it was the murderer. I was so scared!' Even at the memory of the fear that she had felt, Chris couldn't stop shaking. 'And so, when I realized it wasn't, when I realized it was Andy, I was so relieved, so glad to see him, that, at first,' Chris's voice sank to a whisper, 'I didn't resist him.'

'That's what I mean, Chris.' Anna felt her anger rising again. 'Why can't you see it? You were relieved, you were glad, because you trusted him. Why shouldn't you? And what does he do? Sees that as a green light and goes right ahead and rapes you. Terrific.'

'You think it'd be wrong not to do anything about it. That's that you're saying, isn't it?'

'Yes. He shouldn't be allowed to get away with it. You should . . .'

Anna paused, some of her anger ebbing away into uncertainty. It was easy to tell her what she ought to do but imagine the fuss it would cause if Chris did report it. If she was in Chris's place, would she do it?

'What? I should what?'

'Well,' Anna said at last, 'I think you should do something about it, but it's not up to me, is it? In the end it's up to you. You'll have to decide what to do.'

'I can't do it, Anna,' Chris whispered, turning away. 'I'd feel so ashamed if everybody knew.'

Anna forced Chris round so that she could see her face. 'Listen to me, Chris.' She took the other girl by the

162

shoulders and shook her. 'Are you listening to me? You mustn't feel that. You've done nothing wrong. It's him that should be feeling the shame, not you!'

'But perhaps they're all like that,' Chris said miserably, 'perhaps that's just the way it is.'

'No!' Anna shook her head vehemently. 'That's not right either. Mark isn't for a start off. And Nick Stephens isn't, is he? And,' she stopped for a moment as a new thought suddenly hit her, 'there are other things. Other reasons. What if,' her voice dropped to a whisper, 'what if you're pregnant? What about AIDS?'

Chris stared at her in horror. Pregnant. It was the most obvious thing of all but in her pain and confusion she hadn't even thought about it.

She shook her head, trying to dismiss what Anna was saying.

'Andy doesn't have AIDS,' she hissed. 'Don't be stupid!'

'How do you know?' Anna insisted. 'You can't know for certain. He didn't use anything did he? You have to make sure. That's why you've got to report it.'

The knock at the door made them both start. Anna got up slowly to answer it.

'Hi, you two. It's only me,' Ms Steadman said as she came into the room, 'just checking that everything's all right. Also . . .' she hesitated, massaging her forehead, 'it's about Andy. Andrew Henderson. I don't want to alarm you Chris, but he's missing. I wondered, well, if either of you had seen him or if you knew anything? So far he's unaccounted for, and we're extremely worried.'

Neither of the girls replied. Ms Steadman stared down at them, puzzled, sensing the tension in the room. There was something badly wrong here. Chris hadn't moved.

163

She just sat on the side of the bed all hunched over, her hands hiding her face. Anna seemed confused, abstracted, very unlike her normal self.

'What's the matter?' Ms Steadman asked. 'Want to tell me about it?'

Chris continued to stare at the floor. Anna shrugged and shook her head in answer to the teacher's enquiry and then went back to studying her fingernails.

Ms Steadman waited, arms folded, wondering if she would get a response. If they were not prepared to tell her what was troubling them, there wasn't much she could do. She could hardly force it out of them if they decided that it was none of her business. She looked at her watch as the silence continued. She didn't like to leave them like this but she was needed elsewhere.

'I'll see you in the morning, then,' she said eventually. 'I really have to go now and see about this Andy business.'

Chris still refused to look at her as Anna said goodnight and accompanied her to the door.

'Ms Steadman wait!'

She turned at the sound of her name. Anna was sprinting after her down the corridor.

'There's something we want to tell you.'

She followed the girl back into the room.

'Yes, what is it?'

'It's about Andy,' Anna said, ignoring Chris's frantic whispering, and closed the door.

Chapter 28

When he first left Chris's room, Andy felt nauseous and his right leg was shaking out of control. He had to lean against the wall to get a hold on himself. He concentrated on the part of his mind that still functioned bright and luminous, instructing him to work for his own survival, to shut everything else out. There was time to pick up his pack, make it back to the bivouac, not be missed. He made his way to the top of the stairs and stood there, tuning his hearing to every sound in the house, picking each one up to filter it out. Getting in had been easy, an arrangement with Gary. He had not expected the police there, that was a bit heavy duty, but it shouldn't be so hard to get past them. They were there to stop people getting in, not getting out. Anyway, they weren't looking for him. They weren't looking for a kid, right? The real problem was Steadman. He silently descended the stairs and willed her to stay put, wherever she was.

Then he was out, moving from shadow to shadow, getting away from the house. The chalk mark he had left gleamed in the moon light and he shouldered his pack, following the narrow steep pathway back to the high hills and the rest of the group. With every step it would be easier to pretend that he had never left them, that he had spent the whole night roaming around. It had not happened, she dreamt it, she had been hallucinating. He hadn't even been there, he hadn't even been back there, so it couldn't have happened, whatever she said. That was the way to deal with it, it had always worked in the past so why not now? When stuff was done, gear disappeared, got broken, or when things happened to people, it could never be put down to Andy. He was never around.

The path forked in front of him. He didn't remember this. He stopped, suddenly uncertain, searching for clues as to what to do. He would have liked to use his torch but he couldn't risk that. It was hard to work out which was the right way, in a world where everything was shades of black and grey and there weren't any reference points. He struck off to the right. What did it matter? Distance mattered, not direction. He was exhausted, his legs felt like lead. All he wanted to do was get out his sleeping bag and crawl into it. He'd shut his eyes and shut it out. Time would go back, fading her voice, so he would no longer hear her saying it over and over again. He couldn't remember now if she had hissed it or whispered it or if she had said it at all but the words were in his head now, telling him how much she hated him.

He must have hurt her badly to make her feel that way. Usually he hurt people because they were weak and deserved it or they had it coming, because of something they had done or said. But he couldn't make Chris fit into that. She was not weak, she was not any of those things, she was someone you could respect. It wasn't just that she was attractive, that had become less important the more he got to know her. She was much more than that. He had liked her intelligence and honesty, found her interesting and funny, good to be with. He'd been thinking about her all the time. He'd wanted her for his girlfriend so they could be together constantly, because he loved her. He really believed he did.

'You've got a strange way of showing it, mate.' Mark's voice sounded, mocking, in his head. 'What are you? A caveman? I could have told you, girls like her don't go for that kind of shit. And what you're doing now, running away, that ain't going to solve anything.'

He stood on the path, no longer able to shut it all away in some part of his head. He'd hurt her, done something terrible to her. He could not block out the memory of her tear-stained face, close to his, distorted by loathing. He had not meant it to happen like that, but how was Chris, how were other people, going to judge it? Sweat ran clammy cold down his back under his pack and his stomach contracted with dread. He stumbled on, losing the path, following the contours of the hill, zig zagging through a dark sea of bracken. He went through the tall fronds, arms held high, wiping tears and flies from his face with the sleeve of his jacket. He stopped to clear his nose like he would on the football field. There was more light. The stars in the east shone weakly now, like daytime street lamps. Above him the sky was still a clear deep blue but in the west clouds massed above the mountains. There was rain coming.

He made his way up to where the vegetation was more sparse. The covering of soil had been stripped away here to show the bones of the landscape and a thin ledge of a path skirted the side of the mountain. As he edged round he looked out and down to get some idea of where he was. He tripped over something and fell on to a large flat rock that stuck out in front of him and sat there, shaking. He couldn't go any further, and anyway, what was the point? He looked again. There was the house right down there below him. He'd walked for hours, trying to get away, and come back on himself in a great big circle.

He shifted his foot, reaching down for what had caught round his boot and tripped him. He pulled up a thin tangled strap and stared for a second without recognition.

167

He was holding the binoculars Gary had lost. There was the school stencil. He examined them in the gathering light. The casing was battered and the lenses were cracked and fissured. How did they get up here?

He approached the cliff behind him, studying it for a moment, and then he flinched. His hand went up to his face, to his head, and he glanced at the sky, puzzled. Rain clouds were building in the west but above him was perfectly clear, yet something was raining down, first one drop splashed on him and then another. He withdrew his hand and looked at it. The liquid smeared across his palm, dark and tacky. He sniffed at it, Christ it was blood. He moved quickly out of the way and looked up. There was a ledge above him, a jutting lip of rock. Vegetation tufted out like human hair, that was where it was coming from. He stood still, fighting down the impulse to go, to get away as fast as he could. He knew he would have to climb. It would be a hard one with that overhang, and he was terrified of what he might find, but he had to do it. He started up the face. Something was bleeding badly up there and whatever it was might still be alive. It could be an animal, but it could be a climber or even someone off the bivouac.

Andy had never seen a body before, but he knew straight away that the guy was dead. Even so, he squatted down and felt in his neck for a pulse. The skin was still faintly warm but there was nothing. The guy lay sprawled out as if in sleep but his jaw hung down, and his eyes, sunk into their sockets, stared fixed and unseeing. It must be him, Andy thought, the one they were looking for. There was a thin blade, crusted and stained, lying by his side. Flies were already crawling on him, on his forearms and hands. Andy brushed them away but they only came back again.

He took off his coat and laid it over the body. The emotions that occurred to him were strange, not what he would have expected to feel. The guy was dead, but he looked so young. It was not the presence of death, it was the absence of life that most shocked him. I can't get him down by myself, he thought, I'll have to go and tell someone. I can't leave him up here like this.

He leaned out over the edge, assessing the best way back, relieved to concentrate his mind on practical details. He turned around. It would be safer to climb to the top and find another way down. He stood up. He had found a reason to return. It couldn't help him deal with what he'd done down there, but it made it easier for him to go back and face it.

Chapter 29

Wainwright was standing at the window, watching the steady fall of rain, when W.D.C. Townsend came into the room.

'Any sign of the lad yet?' she asked.

'Henderson?' He turned round. The two nights without sleep were beginning to catch up on him. He rubbed at the dark uneven growth that stubbled his cheeks and chin. 'No. He's still out there somewhere. And with Saunders still at large,' he shook his head, 'what a balls up. Bit of a nightmare scenario all round.'

Wendy Townsend nodded her agreement. Right from the start nothing had gone right with this investigation, nothing had gone as they'd planned.

'What's happening with the other kid, the girl?' he asked after a moment. 'Thanks for taking that over, Wendy. I appreciate it.'

If she felt any resentment at being sidelined into women and domestic, she didn't show it. Her assessment was cool and professional as she told him the girl's story. She'll go far, he thought, with all this equal opportunities business, farther than me, probably.

'It's all up to the local police now,' she finished. 'It's their patch after all. It's up to them what happens next.'

'That'll depend on the lad's side of it.' Wainwright sat down, stretching his legs.

'Well, he'd be stupid to deny he was there or that he

had intercourse, the doctor with the mountain rescue has seen her, we've got the forensic.'

'Yeah,' Wainwright agreed, 'but it all comes down to consent. He could say that she knew he was coming back. That they had some sort of prior arrangement. Her mate, what's her name – Anna – wouldn't be there, so they could spend the night together. And he assumed, therefore, that she was willing for it to happen, but then he got a bit carried away. He was a bit rough with her and what with it being her first time she freaked out. If he claims that he really believed she gave her consent . . .'

'There are definite signs of assault, though,' Wendy Townsend interjected, 'and *she* certainly doesn't think she gave her consent.'

'Like you said,' he sighed, 'it's up to the locals. But they know he's her boyfriend and what with his age and no previous . . .' Wainwright shrugged, and leaned towards her. 'Look. We know ourselves, these kind of cases, where the accused and the victim know each other, are going out together, where it's her word against his, it's a real grey area. Difficult to prove, hard to prosecute. Even if it went to court he'd probably get off if he had a good brief.' He sank back in his chair. 'Depends on the girl, to some extent. On how determined she is.'

Wendy Townsend's mouth set in a straight line. 'She seems pretty determined to me. And her teacher, Ms Steadman, is going to be very supportive. She's already seeking advice, she's got a friend who works in a Rape Crisis Centre.'

Wainwright turned his eyes up to the ceiling. 'She bloody would have. Fully paid-up feminist, isn't she? I hope she realizes that what's happened so far is nothing compared to what'll happen if it goes to court. Does she really want the girl to go through all that? I'm just glad

I'm not dealing with it. In this sort of rape case quite often nobody wins. Both become the accused, both end up as victims.'

W.D.C. Townsend did not reply. She did not necessarily share his opinion or agree with his observations about Liz Steadman but, since it would not be their case, there was little point in arguing about it.

'Time to put the crystal ball away,' he said, echoing her last thoughts, 'we've done all we can and our job is getting Saunders, not this.' The radio in his pocket bleeped into action, he reached to answer it. 'Wainwright here. What is it?'

The call sign was lost in crackling distortion but the message was clearly audible even through the clatter of helicopter noise.

'. . . there's someone down on the ground, above him now, maintaining position, going in for a closer look . . .'

Andy froze in the terrifying thunder of noise. Fear swept over him in waves like the rushing wind from the powerful blades turning above him.

'STAY WHERE YOU ARE.'

There was no choice but to obey the huge disembodied voice that boomed around him. He stood, head down and trembling, as a helmeted figure in blue overalls abseiled down and ran towards him.

'Clive Alan Saunders . . .' The man shouted to him above the row made by the rotor blades.

'No.' His voice cracked high and panicking. 'That's not my name! My name is Andrew Henderson.'

The man swore to himself and turned away, speaking into the mouth piece attached to his helmet.

'It's not him. Sorry, skipper. It's that kid, Henderson. Do you want him brought in?'

In the house, Detective Inspector Wainwright swore back.

'Yes, we want him but I want you to continue the search. The weather's closing in and helicopter time costs money. Give me your position and I'll send someone to pick him up.'

'He seems pretty scared.'

'Good. Bloody trouble he's caused he should be,' Wainwright replied. 'Tell him to stay where he is now or I'll chop his balls off personally.'

The policeman laughed and relayed the message to Andrew. But when his voice came back to Wainwright it had changed. It was charged with urgency, excited.

'Say what?' it said. 'Did you catch that, skipper? He says he's seen something. Could be Saunders. He says he's seen a body.'

Chapter 30

'What's going on, Liz?' Mike Peters asked, when she came back into the room. She was even paler than before and her face was etched with tiredness. 'Have they found Andy?'

'Yes, they've found him, and they're bringing him in,' Liz Steadman replied. 'But that's not all of it. I thought it was bad enough before, it's getting worse by the minute.'

'For Christ's sake, Liz. What is?'

'Andy. Somehow he's managed to get himself mixed up in all this other business.' Liz pinched the bridge of her nose and shut her eyes for a second. 'And it sounds pretty horrific. There's a body up there on the mountain, and he found it. They think it must be Saunders.'

'What? Jesus. That's terrible.' Mike Peters blinked hard and stared at her, eyes wide, trying to register this last piece of unwelcome information. 'What's going to happen now? What sort of state is he going to be in?'

'I don't know,' Liz said, shaking her head. 'Pretty shocked, I should imagine. Christ, you've got to hand it to Henderson, this time he's certainly landed himself right in it.'

'What's going to happen about, you know, him and Chris O'Neill?'

Liz Steadman shrugged. 'I don't know. It's up to the police now. And they aren't saying anything, other than that they'll be taking a statement from him.'

'How is she?'

'Bearing up, considering,' Liz replied, 'but what she's really thinking, feeling inside, I hate to think.'

'Where is she?'

'Up in her room.'

'By herself?' Peters asked, surprised.

'Yes. She wanted to be on her own for a bit.'

'This is a real mess, isn't it?' Peters ran his hands through his hair. 'Couldn't we have sorted it ourselves? Why the hell did you have to go and involve the police?'

Liz looked away from him, biting her lip. How many people were going to say that to her? As if, somehow, it was not the rape that was wrong, it was reporting it. As if the best thing to do once something like that happened was to sweep it under the carpet.

'What else could I do?' she said, when she could trust her voice. 'Once I was told about it, I couldn't ignore it, pretend it hadn't happened, could I? It's a serious criminal offence, Mike, and it happened right here, while I was in charge and the police were on the premises. And then he did a runner. How were we supposed to find him without police help?'

'Yeah, I know,' he sighed, 'you had no choice. Sorry.' He turned his hands up in despair. 'I keep thinking. If I'd listened to you in the pub we never would have gone on the bivouac. And I should have kept them together, if I'd noticed he'd gone.' He shook his head. 'I feel terrible about it.'

'It's not your fault,' she replied quietly. 'I'm just as much to blame as you are. I didn't stop you from going. I was responsible for what was happening in the house.' She massaged her temples, closing her eyes. 'I could go on and on. I feel responsible for the whole damned business.'

They sat in silence, staring out at the rain. Then Peters shook himself and looked at his watch.

'What's done is done. There's no point going over and over it,' he said, pushing himself up. 'We'll have to think about driving back. Have you considered that? We're way behind schedule already.' He reached for the phone. 'Better get down to practicalities. Contact the school, tell them there's been complications, let them know we'll be late.' He hesitated before punching in the number. 'D'you think you ought to have a word with the Head, about Andy and Chris? It might be better coming from you and it might be an idea to find out what he thinks we ought to do, I mean, about the parents and so on.'

Liz Steadman held her hand out for the phone.

'You better give it to me, then,' she said.

Chapter 31

Chris stood at the window after her shower, towelling her hair and watching them recover Saunders' body. It was the final act in someone else's drama and they were all witnesses. The helicopter hovered, tearing at and shredding off bits of the thin ragged clouds that now covered the hilltops, and men strung down from it, manoeuvring a stretcher and getting it into position. It was like having a film going on right outside your window. People stood in the rain, like extras waiting to be called, in their bright blue and orange kagouls. It was the guy they'd been looking for, one whisper said, killed himself up there on the mountain. Andy found him, added another. That must have been terrible for him, Chris thought. He must be back in the house now, she wondered what he was feeling. She had to stop herself from doing this. Thinking about him hurt too much. It was too confusing. Inside her there was a raw ragged wound and at the moment it was better to leave it unexplored.

Chris turned her attention to the people on the ground. Dave and Gary stood bareheaded, nodding down at Natalie, agreeing with her about something. Mark was pointing up at the mountainside. What were they saying? Were they making Andy into some kind of hero? And what would that make her? She wanted to know but she couldn't go down there to find out. She drew back, as Mark draped his arm round Anna in casual affection, feeling frozen, unique in her separateness.

She had exiled herself in her room because she knew her presence would disturb them and she could not stand their gaze. Either they would see her as the victim of something they didn't want to think about or they would look at her with accusations already forming in their heads.

But neither could she stay here. Up here on her own she felt in the middle of what had happened. She seemed to hear the different voices of those who had questioned her through the night, expertly probing, obtaining every little detail by their gentle, insistent interrogation. The worst thing had been telling Ms Steadman, her face burned at the memory. She'd rather tell a room full of perfect strangers than go through that again.

'It doesn't matter, ultimately, what happens to him,' Ms Steadman had said at the end of their interview. 'What's important to me is what happens to you. You'll have help and support, don't worry about that. You'll have all the support we can get. You won't be on your own in this. But,' she'd paused before going on, 'when the worst possible thing happens, you've got to learn to live with it. In the end it's all you can do. You'll survive. You're strong, Chris.' Then her dark eyes had searched Chris's face and some of the certainty had dropped from her voice as she added, 'Telling the police was the right thing to do. You do believe that, don't you?'

Chris had stared back, sensing that Ms Steadman wanted some sort of reassurance from her. Reassurance that Chris, at the time, was not ready to give. It was all too near, too frightening.

She finished dressing and, for the first time since it happened, she looked at herself in the mirror. Apart from being pale and the dark smudges under her eyes, she really didn't look any different. She was strangely surprised that the mirror did not reflect the changes she felt inside. It was odd, not to feel the same, to feel older than your own reflection. She was lost for a time, like when she was a small child and would gaze for hours, sitting at her mother's dressing table, trying to see who in the world she could be. You can't stay up here for the rest of your life, she said at last. She brushed her hair and straightened the collar of her shirt, and applied a little blusher to disguise her pallor. You'll have to face it sometime. You might was well go down now and get on with it.

She met him at the turn of the stairs. His clothes were patched with mud and wet, his hair slicked down, darkened by the rain, his face dirt-streaked, haggard. She knew by his quick glance away and the sudden colour staining his cheeks that the police had spoken to him about last night and what had happened between them. They were not supposed to meet. They both knew it. Those few moments of shocking intimacy meant that, now, they should not even speak to each other. He tried to pass but she blocked him, he was forced to look at her.

'I'm sorry . . .' he started to say.

'I don't want to hear it.' She held up her hands to deflect the words. 'Even if you are it's too late for that now and, anyway, I don't forgive you.'

'What have you told them?'

'I've told them the truth,' Chris said.

'And really landed me in it.'

'What did you expect, Andy?' she said quietly. 'What did you think was going to happen?'

'I don't know,' he muttered, his eyes sliding away from hers. He was unable to match the anger he saw there, or the determination.

'What do you think I should do?' He was forced to look at her again, appeal to her.

'Telling the truth might help. But,' she shrugged her shoulders in resignation, 'you won't will you? I know you, and anyone who knows you would say the same thing, you'd say anything to save your own skin.'

'What if I do tell them the truth?' he said, his voice rising. Her last words had stung through his fatigue and feigned indifference. 'Just supposing I do tell them. What do you think will happen?'

'I don't know,' she said, shaking her head.

It was not up to them now, was it? What he'd done had changed everything, taken it out of their control, out of their hands. When you did it like that, what was supposed to be a private act, had public consequences. That was what had horrified her at first, made her want to hide it, pretend it hadn't happened.

'Honestly, Andy,' her eyes filled suddenly and she felt close to tears, 'I didn't tell them in order to get you, to put you in it, whatever you think. They had to practically force it out of me.' She paused, choosing the next words carefully. 'I'm not even saying it's all your fault. I was stupid, naive, to trust you, but that's not a criminal offence, is it?'

'And what I did is, that's what you're saying, isn't it? You've got the police involved and they're going to do me for this. I hope you're satisfied.'

'Do you really think I want that?' She stopped and considered him for a moment. 'But . . .'

'But what?'

'I know what you're thinking.'

'Oh, yeah?' he said, reddening under her stare. 'And what am I thinking?'

Her mouth twisted in a slight bitter smile. 'It would've

been better if she'd kept her mouth shut. Why did she have to go and tell them anything.'

'Well, why did you?' he finally had to ask her.

'I thought about keeping it quiet,' she said, looking away. 'I didn't want to tell them, not to start with.' Her eyes were back on him now, suddenly intense. 'What happened was wrong. Keeping quiet about it might help you, but it's not going to help me, is it? Not saying anything doesn't change it or make it go away. It happened, Andy, and it's something I'm always going to have to live with.'

She moved away then, no longer seeking to bar his way. He stepped past her and on up the stairs, her final words ringing after him.

All Pan books are available at your local bookshop or newsagent, or can be ordered direct from the publisher. Indicate the number of copies required and fill in the form below.

Send to: Pan C. S. Dept
               Macmillan Distribution Ltd
               Houndmills Basingstoke RG21 2XS
or phone: 0256 29242, quoting title, author and Credit Card number.

Please enclose a remittance* to the value of the cover price plus: £1.00 for the first book plus 50p per copy for each additional book ordered.

*Payment may be made in sterling by UK personal cheque, postal order, sterling draft or international money order, made payable to Pan Books Ltd.

Alternatively by Barclaycard/Access/Amex/Diners

Card No.

Expiry Date

Signature:

Applicable only in the UK and BFPO addresses

While every effort is made to keep prices low, it is sometimes necessary to increase prices at short notice. Pan Books reserve the right to show on covers and charge new retail prices which may differ from those advertised in the text or elsewhere.

NAME AND ADDRESS IN BLOCK LETTERS PLEASE:

....

Name _____

Address _____

_____

_____

_____

6/92